MIND.

MONEY.

MATTER.

PAN-AFRICAN INTEGRATION
IN THE 21ST CENTURY

EMEKE E. IWERIEBOR

Printed in the United States of America

Library of Congress Control Number: 2020910892
ISBN: Softcover   978-1-64908-232-9
                eBook   978-1-64908-231-2

Republished by: PageTurner Press and Media LLC
Publication Date: 08/03/2020

To order copies of this book, contact:

PageTurner Press and Media
Phone: 1-888-447-9651
order@pageturner.us
www.pageturner.us

To Philip Iyare Iweriebor,
The Miner
The Entrepreneur
The Unstoppable
A Just Leader
A Resilient Spirit
My Hero
My Father.

To Alice Titi Iweriebor,
A Potter's Hand
A Gentle Spirit
A Kind Heart
A Financial Manager
A Resilient Spirit
My Heroine
My Mother.

CONTENTS

PART III

FINANCING AFRICA

PART IV

INDUSTRIALISING AFRICA

PART V

MINDWARE IN AFRICA

PREFACE

Mind. Money. Matter - Pan – African Integration in the 21st Century has been influenced by my deep and abiding interest in Africa's economic, social and political renaissance as well as my first-hand observations and experiences in the implantation and nurturation of banking institutions across Africa. Broadly, the book provides a comprehensive and experiential insight on doing business successfully, in Africa. In my work and sojourn around Africa, I noticed an interesting and significant trend, and perhaps an unintended consequence of economic activities. As I tried to capture in the book, African businesses are integrating Africa. The firms do not rely on, or depend on, government. They take the lead. They take action. On the other hand, national governments, through direct policies and actions, are also creating structures and instituting measures for the expansion of companies in African countries. The outcomes of some of these measures, though inadvertent, have been positive. A good example is the significant increase in the minimum capital of banks from about $20m to almost $200m in Nigeria in 2006. Its immediate impact was to capacitize and embolden banks in Nigeria to expand across borders and take on larger and potentially transformational initiatives and transactions. Overall, in this new wave of integration in Africa, the people are far ahead of their governments.

African firms have begun to independently explore opportunities and expand into other African countries. The veil of uncertainty is being lifted.

Another pattern has been the increasing use of "Africa" in the business lexicon and legal names of companies and institutions on the continent.

Besides the growth and expansion of businesses within the continent, my postulation is that the framework of NEST – films, music, entertainment and sports, and the activities of religious organisations and other emerging economic and social sectors – represent new and strong expressions of integration in Africa.

The platform of play has expanded, from one country to fifty- five countries, with over a billion people participating.

Join me on this voyage of discovery, rediscovery and action as we *build Africa.*

Emeke E. Iweriebor

INTRODUCTION:
THE QUEST FOR PAN-AFRICAN
DEVELOPMENT AND INTEGRATION[1]

Political Roadmap

Pan-African integration has been an issue of abiding interest to Africans on the continent and in the diaspora for about two centuries. However, this realisation became urgent and defined during the struggles for independence by African nationalists and was supported by the pan-Africanist movements in the diaspora led by Marcus Garvey, George Padmore, C.L.R. James, Henry Sylvester-Williams, W.E.B. Du Bois, Paul Robeson and many others. Though with different strands, the pan-African leaders sought independence for African colonies and, in varying degrees, were interested in unifying Africans in the continent and all people of African descent. These initiatives culminated in pan-African conferences in Paris in 1919; in London, in 1921; in Brussels, in 1921; in London and

---

1   This introduction was based on the ideas in Pan-Africanism: A Survey from Emergence to Renascent Africa in *Pan-Africanism, Globalisation and Renascent Africa, July 2016* by Ehiedu E.G. Iweriebor

Lisbon, in 1923; in New York, in 1927; the well-heralded and well-attended pan-African conference in Manchester, UK, in 1945; and the two conferences hosted by a newly-independent Ghana, in April and December 1958.

Some leaders even advocated for continental unification. Kwame Nkrumah, in his speech at Ghana's Independence Day celebrations in 1957, posited that "our independence is meaningless unless it is linked up with the total liberation of Africa"[2]. Similarly, Julius Nyerere of Tanzania in his book, *African Freedom,* argued that African unity would facilitate self-governance and the appropriate utilisation of resources for the benefit of Africans.

Building Institutional Frameworks

Other early institutional manifestations of pan-African integration were the set-up of the Organisation of African Unity (OAU) in 1963, and the creation of Regional Economic Communities (RECs) viz the Arab Maghreb Union (AMU), the Common Market for Eastern and Southern Africa (COMESA), the Community of Sahel-Saharan States (CEN-SAD), the East African Community (EAC), the Economic Community of Central African States (ECCAS), the Economic Community of West African States (ECOWAS), the Inter-Governmental Authority on Development (IGAD), and the Southern African Development Community (SADC).

The creation of the African Economic Community in 1991, and African Union in 2002, were also geared, among other

---

2   Ghana's Independence from Her Colonial Masters - Can It Be Meaningless? By
    G.D. Zaney in www.ghana.gov.gh

things, towards integrating Africa. The AU's Agenda 2063, also outlined strategic projects that would enhance economic development and pan-African integration. They include[3]:

- Integrated High Speed Train Network
- Africa Virtual and E-University
- African Commodity Strategy
- Annual African Forum
- Continental Free Trade Area
- African Passport and free movement of people
- Grand Inga Dam Project
- Pan-African E-Network
- Silencing the Guns
- African Outer Space Strategy
- Single Air-Transport Network
- Continental Financial Institutions

OHADA[4] – Transforming the Business Landscape in Africa

OHADA, which derives from its French acronym *Organisation pour l'harmonisation en Afrique du droit des affaires*, meaning the "Organisation for the Harmonisation of Business Law in Africa", is a pan-African organisation created on 17 October 1993 in Mauritius and with headquarters in Yaounde, Cameroon, and focused on streamlining corporate laws in member states. Its mission is succinct. It aims to harmonise business law in Africa in order to guarantee legal and judicial security for investors and companies in its member states. Currently, there are 17 Francophone African member countries – Guinea Bissau,

---

3   Pan-Africanism: A Survey from Emergence to Renascent Africa in *Pan-Africanism, Globalisation and Renascent Africa, July 2016* by Ehiedu E.G. Iweriebor

4   See http://www.ohada.org on the history, mission, and activities of OHADA.

Senegal, Central African Republic, Mali, Comoros, Burkina Faso, Benin, Niger, Côte d'Ivoire, Cameroon, Togo, Tchad, Congo, Gabon, Equatorial Guinea, Guinea and DR Congo (DRC). In a reflection of its non-restrictive ambition, while OHADA's current membership composition is actually all in Francophone Africa, its constitutive documents refer to African Union states or any other state invited to join. In essence, it considers itself as pan-African and an international organisation. OHADA deploys its Uniform Acts, its business laws which are required to be adopted by – and apply to – all member countries equally. The Uniform Acts represent the legal fulcrum upon which the business activities and practices of OHADA are driven and implemented. To date, there are ten Uniform Acts on various aspects of business law and commercial practice in member countries as follows:

i. Insolvency Law
ii. General Commercial Law
iii. Organising Securities
iv. Contracts for the Carriage of Goods by Road
v. Commercial Companies and Economic Interest Groups
vi. Law of Cooperative Societies
vii. Organising Simplified Recovery Procedures and Measures of Execution
viii. Arbitration
ix. Mediation
x. Harmonisation of Labour Law (draft)

Among other things, a significant change emanated from the Uniform Act on Commercial Companies and the Economic Interest Group which was adopted in Ouagadougou, Burkina Faso, on 30 January 2014. For the first time, the

Act legally permitted the use of video conference and other telecommunication facilities during board meetings. According to Article 454-1, "If the articles of association so provide, directors who participate in the board meeting by video conference or other means of telecommunications, allowing their identification and guaranteeing their effective participation, may vote orally."[5] The Uniform Acts and the ensuing business liberating guidelines are clearly facilitating business activities remotely and beyond boundaries.

Continental Free Trade Area (CFTA)

The establishment of the Continental Free Trade Area in 2018 was also aimed at the institutionalisation of the processes and mechanisms of integration.

---

5   UNIFORM ACT ON COMMERCIAL COMPANIES AND THE ECONOMIC INTEREST GROUP http://www.ohada.org/attachments/article/537 /AUSCGIE-EN_Unofficial_Translation.pdf

PART I

PERSPECTIVES ON INTRA-AFRICAN TRADE, INTERACTIONS AND INTEGRATION

Chapter One

THE IMPERATIVES OF INTRA-AFRICAN TRADE

In building a developed and industrialised Africa, with an integrated community of over one billion people and an impactful global voice, intra-African trade is an important lever that African countries must constantly pull in a structured and organised manner. Africa's share of global import trade stood at $534 billion or about 3% in 2017, while the share of global merchandise exports amounts to $417 billion, or about 2.4%, out of a burgeoning global import trade of over $17.5 trillion and global export trade of $17.2 trillion[6] respectively, all in 2017.

To accentuate this, Africa's share of this trade declined from 4.6% in 1983 to 2.4% in 2017. Formal and documented trade within Africa hovers around 11.7%, though a significant amount of informal trade takes place within the continent, but

---

6   Global perspectives – who are the leading players? World Trade Statistical Review 2018 by World Trade Organisation in https://www.wto.org/english/res_e/statis_e/ wts2018_e/wts2018chapter05_e.pdf pp.pg 77-79

Table 5.1

Developing economies' merchandise trade by region, 2016-2017

(US$ billion and annual percentage change)

	EXPORTS					IMPORTS				
	Value	Share in world		Annual% change		Value	Share in world		Annual % change	
	2017	2016	2017	2016	2017	2017	2016	2017	2016	2017
Developing economies[a]	7433	42.7	43.2	-5	12	7138	39.9	40.6	-5	13
Latin America	993	5.7	5.8	-4	12	1011	5.9	5.8	-9	8
Developing Europe	189	1.1	1.1	0	11	282	1.5	1.6	-3	17
Africa	417	2.3	2.4	-10	18	534	3.1	3.0	-11	8
Middle East	961	5.2	5.6	-7	18	712	4.4	4.1	-5	1
Developing Asia[a]	4875	28.3	28.3	-5	11	4600	25.0	26.2	-4	16
Memorandum items										
World[a]	17198	100.0	100.0	-3	11	17572	100.0	100.0	-3	11
Developed economies	9247	54.6	53.8	-1	9	10032	58.0	27.1	-1	9
Commonwealth of Independent States, including associate and former member states	518	2.7	3.0	-16	24	402	2.1	2.3	-3	21

Excluding Hong Kong (China) re-exports or imports for re-exports
Source: WTO estimates[a]

well below governmental radar. It is therefore clear that trade, industry and economic activities within the continent must be prioritised as the advantages of proximity, connection and deep historical, economic, trade and cross-cultural understanding of African people must be utilised and maximised. For Africa, an area of focus must be intra-African industry and commerce, given its multiplier effect on economic growth, value addition, supply chain, technological development and integration in the continent. So, rather than a preoccupation with the global trade imbalance and its share of global trade, Africa needs to focus on developing intra-African trade and to continually expand, deepen and organise her economies, as this builds

---

a   Global perspectives – who are the leading players? World Trade Statistical Review 2018 by World Trade Organisation in https://www.wto.org/english/res_e/statis_e/ wts2018_e/wts2018chapter05_e.pdf pp.pg 77-79

local capacity in skills, production and engineering, strengthens competitiveness and leads to overall advanced economic regeneration.

Impediments to Intra-African Trade

The economic philosophy of colonialism centred on the movement of goods and services from the hinterland in colonial territories to coastal ports for onward shipment and delivery to Europe. Therefore, the administrative system, the economic system, the transportation system – roads and railways – and the communication system, were designed to facilitate this movement. This system of commodity exports and imports of processed and finished goods had in-built rigidities which continue to this day. Even the educational system was geared towards supporting the colonial administration, with insufficient focus on science, technology, engineering, mathematics, medicine, law, financial services, etc.

Factors that Make Intra-African Trade Imperative

The African Development Bank (AfDB) highlights the fact that there are 15 landlocked countries (now 16, including South Sudan, Africa's newest independent country) out of a total 55 sovereign African countries.[7] I prefer to describe them as *land-linked* countries, given their linkages. Without direct access to the sea, these land-linked countries have no other option but to collaborate with their neighbours to get the wheel of industry and commerce running at home. Tchad, Zambia, Ethiopia, Uganda, Burkina Faso and Mali are, in fact, poster land-linked countries.

---

7   Mbekeani. African Development Bank Group. Pp.17 -31

Tchad

Tchad, for instance, has borders with five countries – Nigeria, Niger, Cameroon, Sudan and Libya. With a landmass of 1,284 sq. km, the three nearest ports to N'Djamena are the ports in Douala in Cameroon, Lagos in Nigeria and Cotonou in Benin, which are 1,700 km, 1,900 km and 2,000 km[8] away respectively. The port in Calabar, Nigeria, could also have been developed to facilitate international trade with Tchad and commercial activities between Nigeria and Tchad. In addition to good neighbourliness, how does Tchad ensure that there are adequate roads, railways or other transport infrastructure to move man and material from these ports to N'Djamena, the capital, and to the hinterland and other parts of the country? The nation-states of the Lake Tchad Basin – Nigeria, Niger, Tchad, and Cameroon – must therefore develop an integrated economic model, leveraging on the proximity and resources of the region and the infrastructural opportunities within the countries. As a starting point, a bridge or railway should be built over Lake Tchad while railways or motorable roads should be built between Cameroon and Tchad, and between N'Djamena, in Tchad, and Maiduguri, in Nigeria, respectively.

Zambia

Zambia is an interesting study on being a land-linked country. It has borders with eight countries – Angola, DR Congo, Malawi, Mozambique, Tanzania, Namibia, Botswana and Zimbabwe. The country therefore has a responsibility towards good neighbourliness. The country has to rely on multi-modal

---

8   Copperbelt Outlook 2014/2015- Mining in Zambia and Democratic Republic of Congo pp.11

transportation means to execute and facilitate regional and international trade and industry. My personal experience in Zambia brought into bold relief the urgency and imperative of deepening intra-African trade. As CEO, United Bank for Africa (UBA), CES (Central, East and Southern) Africa, while developing business for our Kitwe branch, I had travelled from Lusaka to Ndola, and then Kitwe in the Copperbelt Province, with Abba Bello, later CEO of Nigerian Export-Import Bank and, at that time, Country CEO of UBA Zambia. The Copperbelt Province is in southern Zambia. To get to Copperbelt, we traversed through kilometres of good but winding roads, passing Ndola, then on to Kitwe and Chingola, and bypassing Luanshya and other towns, seeing several open copper pits and mines. Even more impressive is the fact that the Copperbelt Province in Zambia actually lies astride Katanga Province in DR Congo, with lodes of copper on both sides of the border. While Zambia is well-known for its copper resources, much less is said of DR Congo's copper resources.

Mining is critical to the economy of DR Congo, as it generates over 80% of the export revenue of the country while copper production, specifically, rose by 200% from 500,000 mt in 2005 to 1,500,000 in 2016, thereby contributing significantly to government revenues and facilitating economic growth. By 2017, copper production had grown by 6.7% and reached 1.09 million mt.[9]

I wanted to explore how we could maximise business opportunities on both sides of the border considering that we were operating in both DR Congo and Zambia. So I went

9   Congo's 2017 copper output up 7ct, cobalt by 15pct – industry in www.reuters.. com/africa-mining-congo-2017; February 7, 2018

to Kasumbalesa, the border town between both countries to see intra-African trade in action. We drove from Ndola to Kitwe and then to Kasumbalesa, a distance of over 150 km. I was astounded by the sight of hundreds of 18-wheeler trucks stationed at the border crossing at Kasumbalesa, freighting goods to and from East Africa, to Southern Africa and beyond. The upgraded border station has witnessed higher carrying capacity from about 400 trucks to about 900 trucks crossing both ways daily.[10] This modern one-stop gateway was financed by the Development Bank of Southern Africa for $25m.[11]

I explored how to turn this logistics nightmare to financial products – a supply chain opportunity and an African trade gateway. It became clear to me that facilitative regional and cross-border infrastructure will make an impact and create opportunity for intra-African trade and economic development across frontiers in the continent. Perhaps thinking along this line, the government of DRC, in May 2018, opened a dry port at Kasumbalesa.

---

10 Mofat Chazingwa in allafrica.com http://allafrica.com/stories/201510220168.html
11 ibid.

Chapter Two

BREAKING DOWN NON-TARIFF BARRIERS

The East African Community (EAC) is the regional economic bloc of East Africa, consisting of Burundi, Kenya, Rwanda, South Sudan, Uganda and Tanzania. South Sudan, the newest and 54th independent African State, became a member in April 2016, after applying for membership in 2011, soon after gaining independence on 9 July 2011.

The EAC has made concerted efforts to eliminate non-tariff barriers impeding regional trade, and facilitate trade and ease of access within the community through, among other things, the single-entry visa (which allows access to multiple countries in the region with visa obtained in one of the countries) and the one-stop border posts (OSBPs). The "OSBP activities are streamlined to maximise efficiency. In this case, travellers will stop only once at the country of destination where their travel and other documents will be stamped at exit (by an official from the traveller's country of origin) and entry (by an official from the traveller's country of destination) at the same time. The officials will be seated next to each other, thus the 'One Stop'."[12]

The EAC, which has about 150 million people, has already built twelve modern OSBPs in the community while several others are under construction. The modern border posts recognise that there is interdependence in the region and these initiatives enhance intra-community trade and economic integration. In February 2016, the first OSBP in the EAC was formally declared open by ministers from Kenya and Tanzania in Holili/Taveta on the Kenya-Tanzania border. The OSBP, which was financed at a cost of about $12 million, provided by Trade Mark East Africa (TMEA), will expectedly reduce both transportation costs and time spent in transit at border crossings by transporters, farmers and businessmen, and facilitate clearance of cargo, movement, cross-border trade and good neighbourliness. To further facilitate economic integration, especially between regions in both countries, the Arusha-Holili-Taveta-Voi Road, then under construction and already in use, was at 75% completion.[13] In the same vein, in June 2016, the OSBP at the Kenya-Ugandan border at Busia was launched. The project, which cost over $13m, will reduce transit times by up to 30%. The border is the busiest border in East Africa, handling more than 780 vehicles crossing the border daily. The Busia OSBP was formally commissioned by Presidents Uhuru Kenyatta of Kenya and Yoweri Museveni of Uganda in February 2018. Importantly, it

---

12 https://www.trademarkea.com/news/trademark-east-africa-hands-over-busia-uganda-one-stop-border-post-facility-operations-start/

13 http://www.eac.int/news-and-media/press-releases/20160227/eac-launches-first-one-stop-border-post-holilitaveta

has led to an 80% reduction in goods transit and clearance time and has also facilitated trade and border regulation between both countries.[14] In the same vein, Presidents John Magufuli and Uhuru Kenyatta jointly declared the Namanga OSBP open in December 2018, making it the 10th OSBP in East Africa.[15] This is important because, in East Africa, transportation costs are among the highest globally.[16] So, measures taken to improve cross-border movement of goods and trade facilitation are beneficial to the economies in the region. For East Africa, and especially for Uganda which is a land-linked country with no direct access to the sea, this is particularly beneficial and a major intervention. Uganda has borders with five countries: Tanzania, Kenya, DRC, South Sudan and Rwanda.

These efforts and concomitant results are indicative of the integrative role of economic activities and trade in development.

African Continental Free Trade Area

The resolution by the African Union (AU) to establish a Continental Free Trade Area is one of the most courageous intentions and decisions by the Union. As conceived by the 18th Ordinary Session of the Assembly of Heads of States of the AU that took place in January 2012 in Addis Ababa, Ethiopia, the Free Trade Area will "create a single continental market for

---

14 http://www.theeastafrican.co.ke/oped/comment/One-stop-border-posts-strengthen-cross-border-trade; Kenya, Uganda trade thrives on one-stop border post in Busia

15 Presidents Uhuru, Magufuli open Namanga One-Stop Border Post https://www.standardmedia.co.ke/article/2001304733/in-pictures-presidents-uhuru-magufuli-open-namanga-one-stop-border-post

16 https://www.businessdailyafrica.com/magazines/Kenya-Uganda-trade-thrives-one-stop-border

goods and services, with free movement of business persons and investments" while expanding "intra-African trade through better harmonisation and coordination of trade liberalisation, and facilitation regimes and instruments across RECs and across Africa in general."[17] After negotiations that commenced in 2015 to harmonise positions, 44 African countries signed the treaty on the formal creation of the African CFTA. The treaty, signed in Kigali, Rwanda on 20 March 2018, marks the creation of the largest free trade and single market in the world by country membership – since the establishment of the World Trade Organisation.[18]

In full operation, the treaty will consist of 55 African Union countries, with a population of 1.2 billion people and a gross domestic product size of over $3.4 trillion. Significantly, the treaty seeks to facilitate business within Africa, as governments will eliminate tariffs on 90% of goods produced in Africa while removing levies, import quotas and other non-tariff barriers over time. The treaty becomes effective when 22 countries ratify the free trade agreement.

Notably, in what is a significant drawback for the AU, ten countries, including Nigeria and South Africa, the two largest economies in Africa did not sign the treaty. For such a defining agreement with the capacity to transform trade, industry and economic relationships within Africa, it was not a good message that the two largest economies in Africa did not sign the agreement at inception. It would have been more appropriate and impactful if the negotiating parties had reviewed and resolved the key differences and onerous terms

---

17 https://au.int/en/ti/cfta/about
18 "African Leaders sign largest trade treaty" in *The East African, 21st March, 2018*

and signed the Agreement, even if this had meant a delay of a few days or weeks. The message and direction of pan-African unity and economic integration would have been stronger and would have reverberated beyond trade and set the continent on a course of economic transformation.

In spite of these teething challenges, more countries continued to sign the Agreement. At the 31st Summit of the Africa Union in Nouakchott, Mauritania, in July 2018, it was announced that with the accession of South Africa, Sierra Leone, Namibia, Lesotho and Burundi, 49 African countries had signed the free trade Agreement while 16 countries had ratified the Agreement. The uptake was progressive. By April 2019, 52 countries had signed the Agreement. With Gambia's ratification of the Agreement, the threshold of 22 countries required for the Agreement to become effective, was reached.[19] Quite significantly and symbolically, and with the resolution of outstanding differences, Nigeria signed the Continental Free Trade Area Agreement at the 12th Extraordinary Summit of the AU in Niamey, Niger Republic, in July 2019. Benin Republic also signed the Agreement, bringing to 54 the total country signatories, out of 55. I expect that Eritrea will, in due course, sign the Agreement.

The signing and ratification of this Agreement by AU member states will open up the continent to economic and commercial

---

19 More countries sign the African free trade area agreement in the East African, July 3, 2018 http//www.theeastafrican.co.ke/business/African-free-trade-area-agreement-signing; "We now have six more AfCFTA ratifications remaining before we reach the magic number of 22 ratifications." AU Press Release January 10, 2019. https://au.int/sites/default/files/pressreleases/35446-pr-pr_003-_stc_ministerial_meeting.pdf, https://www.africanews.com/2019/04/03/afcfta-agreement-to-be-implemented-following-gambia-s-historic-ratification/

opportunities and facilitate increased intra-African trade and industry and the movement of capital and persons. In the course of time, people will become more confident to explore cross-border opportunities and establish engagements, partnerships and businesses within the continent in education, healthcare, manufacturing, commerce, tourism and hospitality, agriculture, mining, telecommunications, technology and even expand the frontiers of finance – one of the increasingly integrated sectors in Africa. These practical initiatives will boost economic activities in Africa.

Chapter Three

BUSINESS INTEGRATION IN AFRICA

An imperceptible and unheralded economic shift is taking place. Africa's corporate businesses are gravitating and coalescing in middle Africa. Large corporates in Southern Africa are moving upwards geographically while large entities from North Africa are moving downwards into West, Central, East and Southern Africa. Businesses in East and West Africa are also migrating to other areas within the continent. An interesting manifestation of this shifting gear is that a growing number of companies in different parts of Africa now include "Africa" in the names of their companies, including those that do not have any presence beyond a single country. This mental shift is clearly indicative of intent, confidence and ambition.

African Torchbearers

While trans-African trade has been a solid part of African history, the emergence of African Torchbearers is a recent phenomenon.

African Torchbearers are African institutions with defined goals to be pan-African in intent and reach, operating under different structures, national and company laws. In defining African Torchbearers, I have developed the following non-exhaustive criteria:

- The majority ownership is African, either by the private sector or public sector state institutions;
- The headquarters of the company or holding company is located in Africa;
- The entity must operate in at least two of the four main linguistic blocs – Anglophone, Francophone, Lusophone and Arab countries;
- The entity must operate in at least ten per cent of African countries, i.e., at least six African countries, or have an evolving pan-African strategy being implemented;
- The entity must meet three out of the four criteria above.

The African Torchbearers listed in this book are Africa-focused. While some of them have operations outside Africa, like MTN in Iran, Afghanistan, etc., Dangote in Vietnam, and *Ethiopian Airlines* with flights to other continents, the focus and direction remains firmly on Africa.

By Geography: North to South

There is also an emerging crop of pan-African firms from North Africa that are now expanding their operations and reach beyond their countries of origin, or even region, to other parts of Africa. Some of them are already large and very successful in their home countries.

Now, it is common to meet companies and executives from Egypt, Libya, Tunisia, Morocco, Algeria and Sudan in Lagos, Johannesburg, Nairobi, Douala, Abidjan, Kinshasa, Ndjamena, Ouagadougou, Conakry, Dakar, Libreville, Accra, Maputo, Niamey, Dar es Salaam, Kampala, Lusaka, Bamako, Addis Ababa, Kigali, etc., in pursuit of opportunities and the extension of commercial frontiers, at international business conferences.

Libya and Morocco have extensively executed this vision. Under the banner of its flagship companies – the Libyan Investment Authority, Libya Foreign Investment Company, The Libyan African Investment Portfolio (LAP) and The Libyan African Investment Company (LAICO) which, amongst other things, owned and ran businesses in different parts of the continent – Libya had a very ambitious programme of setting up international companies operating in different parts of Africa. Its hotel chain, operated under the LAICO and Ledger brands, had operations and properties in ten African countries – Burkina Faso, Central African Republic, Congo Brazzaville, Gambia, Guinea Bissau, Kenya, Tanzania, Tchad, Tunisia and Uganda. There is also the Afriqiyah Airways, one of Libya's state-owned airlines. Founded in 2001, even its name, Afriqiyah, which means "African" in Arabic, was indicative of its focus and ambition. Before the Libyan civil war, it had grown its annual seat capacity from 500,000 to 1.5 million between 2005 and 2010.[20] Years back, I flew the airline between N'Djamena and Douala, and the service was good.

Nonetheless, one of the most successful manifestations of Libya's intra-African economic foray is Oilibya, with operations

---

20 Airline network and analysis. www.anna.aero/2013/10/24/afriqiyah - airways focuses on rebuilding Libya's connectivity/

in 18 countries across Africa where it provides midstream and downstream products and services for retail, commercial aviation and maritime operations. Quite interestingly, the country's political crisis did not disrupt the company's business activities.

Other companies with pan-African credentials and ambitions that are expanding from the North to other parts of the continent include *Air Maroc*, *EgyptAir*, Maroc Telecom, CIMAF, ONEA, Attijariwafa Bank, Bank of Africa, BMCE, etc.

In November 2008, Attijariwafa Bank acquired the banking business of the French Bank, Credit Agricole, in Côte d'Ivoire, Cameroon, Gabon, Senegal, Congo, etc., and created a pan-African banking franchise. CIMAF, a Moroccan cement company, is aggressively expanding in West and Central Africa, with new and upcoming operations in Burkina Faso, Gabon, Côte d'Ivoire, etc. Furthermore, Maroc Telecom has acquired the business of MOOV, Etisalat in Gabon, Côte d'Ivoire, etc.

This has been accentuated by the economic diplomacy of King Hassan IV who has encouraged Moroccan companies to expand beyond Morocco. In fact, in a speech on 20 August 2016, King Mohammed VI stated that Africa would be the "top priority" in the strategic direction of Morocco.[21] The King has formed enduring personal friendships with some Heads of States, especially in Francophone Africa, manifesting in business partnerships. During visits to other African countries, he is usually accompanied by a large delegation of Moroccan business leaders, across different economic sectors. Morocco also re-applied for membership of the African Union, which

---

21 See atlanticcouncil.org

it left voluntarily in 1984, and was readmitted. Furthermore, in a bold and unprecedented move geared towards accelerating its economic integration in Africa, Morocco, though well ensconced in North Africa, announced in 2017, its intention to join the Economic Community of West African States, ECOWAS.

By Geography: South to Central, East and North

Concurrently, the post-apartheid era has witnessed the expansion of some business entities from Southern Africa that had hitherto focused only on South Africa and other countries in the region: Mozambique, Zambia, Botswana, Malawi, Zimbabwe, Lesotho, etc. These companies have confidently begun operations in other African countries. Numerous examples include MTN, VODACOM, Liquid Telecom, Shoprite, Nando's, Woolworth, etc. As at 2017, Shoprite,[22] the South African supermarket chain, which describes itself as "Africa's largest fast-moving consumer goods retail company", with several subsidiaries all over the continent, owned 2,301 corporate stores, with 1,916 (or 83%) in South Africa and 385 (or 17%) in the rest of Africa. It had earlier declared its intention in 2015 to further expand into other African countries, including Nigeria and Angola. In 2015, it projected to open 35 new stores, a 75% increase from the 20 outlets opened in 2014, with Nigeria getting 14 stores within 20 months, and a distribution centre. In 2017, Shoprite

---

22 For more on Shoprite, see, Shoprite Holdings 2017 Integrated Report; https://www.shopriteholdings.co.za; "South Africa's Shoprite finalises entry into Kenya's retail market" By Fredrick Obura; https://www.standardmedia.co.ke/business/article/2001271369/africa-s-biggest-grocer-to-open-seven-branches-in-kenya; South Africa's Shoprite to accelerate African expansion. By TJ Strydom in https://af.reuters.com/article August 18, 2015

opened 72 new supermarkets and planned to open 82 new supermarkets in 2018, in different parts of the continent. The company planned to increase the contribution of its business in Africa, ex-South Africa, from the current 16% of sales and 17% on trading profit in 2017. In 2018, it secured seven sites for its operations in Kenya.

Liquid Telecom, a telecommunications infrastructure company associated with Econet Wireless, a mobile telephone company, which runs a fibre network in Zimbabwe, Lesotho, DRC, Botswana, Zambia, and with operations in Kenya, Uganda and Rwanda provides connectivity to governments, telecommunication companies, banks and many other entities. The company plans to expand its operations to other African countries. It signed a memorandum of understanding with Telecom Egypt for the coordination and extension of their telecommunication infrastructure across Africa. A joint statement put out by the two telecommunication companies stated that "Liquid Telecom will link its network from Sudan into Telecom Egypt's network via a new cross-border interconnection – bringing together a 60,000km network that runs from Cape Town through all the southern, central and eastern African countries, and has now reached the border between Sudan and Egypt."[23]

By Economic Sectors – Financial Services and Banking

Standard Bank, from South Africa, operating as Stanbic, acquired IBTC, a bank in Nigeria, now Stanbic IBTC, and has

---

23 Liquid Telecom and Telecom Egypt to complete pan-African fibre network by Chris Kelly in *https://www.totaltele.com*

also obtained a banking licence in Côte d'Ivoire and Senegal as part of its expansion programme, moving beyond its traditional country operations in Southern and Eastern Africa and Nigeria. This tendency has become unprecedented in banking. From Nigeria, United Bank for Africa (UBA) has announced the intention to expand its operations to 25 African countries. Ecobank, with Lomé, Togo as its group head office, has now expanded to 36 countries in most parts of the continent. Attijariwafa Bank and Bank of Africa, both from Morocco, have expanded to different parts of West, Central and East Africa. Equity Bank started from Kenya and has expanded into all the other countries in the East African Community as well as DRC, with stated ambitions to venture into other African countries.

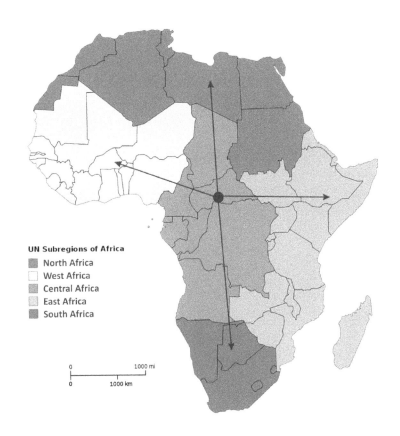

In fact, in May 2019, Equity Bank announced its acquisition of the subsidiaries of Bank ABC in Mozambique, Zambia, Rwanda and Tanzania, further expanding its reach. Afriland from Cameroon, and other banks are also in pursuit of cross-border expansion. What is obvious is that the old home country is not enough. The new home market is now 55 countries with over one billion people.

Manufacturing

In the same vein, Dangote Cement has expanded beyond Nigeria and has operations in ten African countries,[24] with ongoing plans and work to expand to others.

Beyond political declarations, governments, the regional economic communities and other sub and pan-continental organisations should take more structured steps towards promoting businesses operating in multiple African countries and which are integrating Africa. Together, these entities represent the contemporary forces and processes in the promotion and acceleration of pan-African integration in the 21st century.

---

24 http://www.dangotecement.com/wp-content/uploads/2015/11/dangcemsite banner_info321.jpg

PART II

MOBILITY WITHIN AFRICA

Chapter Four

VISA OPENNESS – STATE OF AFFAIRS

Many Africans will be astounded to realise the myriad of challenges faced in obtaining entry visas and permits to some African countries. In fact, one strong brick wall that Africa has faced in building an integrated continent that facilitates the free flow of people, goods, services and capital has been the restriction in the ease of movement of Africans to other countries within the continent. This contradicts the African Union Agenda 2063 which includes, a goal to be "a continent with seamless borders" and its Aspiration 24 which says "the free movement of people, capital, goods and services will result in significant increase in trade and investments among African countries rising to unprecedented levels, and strengthen Africa's place in global trade."[25]

This is necessary, because for Africa to leverage on its demographic dividend of potentially two billion people in 2050,

---

25 Africa Openness Index/Africa Visa Openness Report 2016 - African Development Bank.

with a significantly higher population of 50% below 30 years, it is important that skills, talent and human mobility within the continent be facilitated to enable individuals go to school, work and set up businesses legally in other African countries and without structural impediments. A good way to kick-start this process is to hold African presidents and heads of governments accountable for the elimination of these barriers. Beyond the 30 African countries that committed to the AU Agenda 2063 mandate of eliminating visa restrictions in 2018, and the creation of an African Passport, the African Union must insist that all the 55 independent African countries adhere to the mandate.

Nonetheless, it is important to acknowledge that progress has been made. Today, citizens of ECOWAS and EAC do not require visas to visit any of the sixteen (16) ECOWAS and the six EAC countries, respectively. Rwanda, Mauritius, Ghana, Kenya, Ethiopia and Nigeria have raised the bar by granting visa on arrival to all Africans. While Seychelles, Mali, Uganda, Cape Verde and Togo are among the top five visa-open African countries, Gabon, Libya, Egypt, Equatorial Guinea, and São Tomé and Príncipe have the lowest visa openness ranking.[26] North Africa and Central Africa appear to have the most restrictive visa terms. However, an important agreement instituting visa-free travel by citizens of the six-member countries of CEMAC[27] – Cameroon, Tchad, Gabon, Central African Republic, Republic of Congo and Equatorial Guinea – was reached in November 2017 and announced following a

---

26 Africa Openness Index/Africa Visa Openness Report 2016- African Development Bank.

27 Central Africa: CEMAC Zone – Circulation is Free by Richard Kwang Kometa in www.allAfrica.com October 31, 2017.

meeting of the Heads of States of CEMAC, held in N'Djamena, after twenty-three years of negotiations.

Given the critical importance of the mobility of people, goods, services and capital to economic development, social interaction, political openness and integration, African governments must rapidly enunciate policies and enforce existing protocols on the free movement of Africans within Africa. Concerns on security and migration should be mitigated through an appropriate African Union protocol.

Integration by Foot

Integration by foot refers to the routine actions of Africans in many countries, especially those living in border communities who move across borders to trade and participate in meetings and reunions of family members and friends, religious gatherings, businesses, etc., without much concern with the legalities of formal immigration controls. They are unimpeded by frontiers and official border crossings. The immigration authorities are powerless to stop people without passports, *carte de sejour*, or other travel documents. The people create their own trade routes and foot passages through which they exchange goods and services. They are truly mobile. I have witnessed integration by foot across several borders – at the Seme border, between Nigeria and Benin Republic; at Kasumbalesa, between DRC and Zambia; at Kousseri, between Cameroon and Tchad; at Noe, between Côte d'Ivoire and Ghana; at Aflao, between Ghana and Togo; at Hilla-Condji, between Togo and Benin; at Malaba between Uganda and Kenya; at Busia between Uganda and Kenya; and at Namanga, between Kenya and Tanzania. These activities certainly exist across many other borders.

Though the Mozambique-South African border at Komati is stringent and secure, it does not explain the significant number of Mozambicans in South Africa. This means that in spite of the border security and restrictions, people are still integrating by foot. This observation on cross-border migration and trade made me question the precise validity of the officially reported size of intra-African trade of about 11%, and data on the movement of people within the continent. It was clear to me that there is a significant portion of intra-African trade that is undocumented and, therefore, unrecorded. Otherwise, how does one explain the existence of products, especially fast-moving consumer goods, that are produced in one African country and sold widely and openly in markets and shops in other countries, which were not formally exported by the companies producing them? How does one explain the existence of large markets near borders where goods like automobiles, etc., are sold, but destined for neighbouring countries? The position of Benin Republic as a goods-in-transit market further illustrates the issue. Whenever there is a border closure by the Nigerian government, or there is significant economic downturn in Nigeria, there is an immediate ripple effect in Benin Republic, as the economy stagnates, tax revenues shrink, merchants complain and the government is discomfited. Also, just across the border from Seme, there are large car marts where cars imported into Benin, through the Port of Cotonou, mainly from Europe, are sold. The target market are buyers from Nigeria. Whenever Nigeria faced economic difficulties and the buyers of the cars from Nigeria stopped coming, it led to the near collapse of the business. Furthermore, at a time, most of the frozen fish and rice imported into Benin Republic were headed for Nigeria. The large importers of these goods readily acknowledge that

Lagos, Nigeria is their target market. In fact, some of the frozen fish companies have large cold storage facilities at Seme, the border with Nigeria. The market and destination is clear. These product exchanges do not show up in export and import statistics in Nigeria. In 2016, the government of Benin experienced a significant drop in taxes collected due to the impact of reduced trade between merchants of both countries.[28] In a "Letter of Intent, Memorandum of Economic and Financial Policies, and Technical Memorandum of Understanding" to the IMF, the government of Benin stated that economic growth in Benin witnessed "a significant slowdown" in 2015 due to the "contagion effects" of the recession in Nigeria.[29] Also, Patrice Talon, the President of Benin, in a meeting with Muhammadu Buhari, the President of Nigeria, in Abuja, noted that Nigeria was the "engine room of West Africa". He also admitted that the economic downturn in Nigeria negatively affected most of the countries in West Africa, and he hoped to strengthen the bilateral ties between both countries in trade, economy, energy and education. [30]

Furthermore, some movements of people across borders are not reported in immigration data. But they happen daily as the people weave through and wave at immigration officials. African governments must recognise that the people straddling the borders, on both sides, are usually the same people. African

---

28 Nigeria recession deals blow to smuggling hub Benin Allegresse Sasse and Paul Carsten, Mar 30, 2017 Reuters, and *Benin hit by neighbouring Nigeria's car import ban.* New Vision January 29, 2017. www.newvision.co.ug.

29 https://www.imf.org/external/np/loi/2017/ben/032317.pdf.

30 Economic downturn in Nigeria affecting most African nation – Beninoise ON AUGUST 2, 2016 in https://www.vanguardngr.com/2016/08/nigeria-convert-gas-export-buhari/.

governments must realise that there were historical relationships and trade routes before the existence of modern-day borders.

The story and narrative of the Awori family and dynasty in both Uganda and Kenya, who trace their family history to 1785, is quite instructive of how modern-day international borders massively intervene in the lives and trajectories of families. Besides having successful family members in the church, government and business in both countries, Moody Awori served in government and ended up being the vice president of Kenya in 2003 while Aggrey Awori ran for the Presidency in Uganda in 2001.[31]

Also, the trans-Saharan trade route, extending from West Africa and North Africa through to the Middle East, and many others, existed. Governments must realise that before them, the people were. To strengthen economic integration and development, African governments must consciously and collaboratively develop integrative cross-border road, rail and air travel infrastructure that will facilitate the movement of goods and people. Cross-border trade and movement should be open, welcome and declared rather than undocumented and covert.

---

31 Authors trace Awori dynasty to 18th century patriarch by Margaretta Wa Gacheru in **Business Daily Africa on** MAY 3, 2018 **https://www.businessdailyafrica.com/ lifestyle/books/Authors-trace-Awori-dynasty-to-18th-century-patriarch;** Inside one famous family of scholars and top leaders by Gakiha Weru in **Daily Nation in www.nation.ke/lifestyle.**

Chapter Five

CONNECTING AFRICA

Every society establishes within itself the means of communication appropriate to its time. In earlier epochs, communities used town criers, palace runners and different messaging systems. In these times, the world has moved through the telegraph, the invention of the telephone in 1876 and its continuous improvement, the digitalisation of communication, and the creation of the internet and its whirlpool of information and data. This advancement is now so pervasive that some people "live" on the internet. We are now in an age of virtual reality, artificial intelligence, machine learning and many more mechanisms of communication and engagement. It is all technology-driven. To sustain this new information age, communication and data transmission are required in satellites, fibre networks, underground and underwater cabling systems, traversing thousands of kilometres. In Africa, Glo 1, WACS, EASSY and MainOne are some of the powerful transmission systems that facilitate telephone, broadband and data transmission services within and outside the continent.

Increasingly, education, health, e-commerce and m-commerce, mobile money, etc., also thrive on the internet.

In Africa, the telephone has become the most ubiquitous means of communication. From the cities to the towns and rural areas, the telephone, of the mobile variety, has supplanted all other means of communication. In 2015, mobile penetration had reached 67%, indicating that two in three Africans use a cell phone.[32] Nigeria led the pack with over 174 million active mobile phone users in the country,[33] as at January 2019 – a teledensity of 124%, representing phenomenal growth from less than 500,000 active telephone lines in 2001. This is typical of the transformation of telecommunications in Africa. In the same vein, internet usage in the continent has grown dramatically, the fastest in the world, with over 20% increase in 2017,[34] with Nigeria contributing 103 million mobile internet users as at June 2018.[35] Others like Benin, Sierra Leone, Niger and Mozambique witnessed a 100% growth in internet users in 2017 while Mali grew significantly by 600%.[36] Furthermore, a research conducted by Consumer Insights puts the high online activity by smartphone users for socialising, news, gambling, dating, educational and career pursuits in Nigeria and Kenya at 96%; 93% in South Africa; 91% in Tanzania; and 87% in Uganda. Similarly, online shopping is increasingly common

---

32 http//m.guardian.ng/technology/africas-mobile-phone-penetration-now67/ June 17, 2015, by Adeyemi Adepetun.

33 https://www.ncc.gov.ng/stakeholder/statistics-reports/subscriber-data

34 Digital in 2018: Africa's internet users increase by 20%. Daniel Mumbere www. Africannews.com 6/02/2018.

35 op cit www. ncc.gov.ng - Industry Statistics.

36 Digital in 2018: Africa's internet users increase by 20%. Daniel Mumbere www. Africannews.com 6/02/2018.

place with Nigeria at 64%; South Africa at 62%; Kenya at 57%, and Tanzania at 39%, amongst others.[37] Though, as evidenced above, there are clearly multifarious communication means, we will focus on GSM, and for ease, on an African mobile phone company with a wide cell phone penetration and coverage in the continent.

Y'ello Africa – MTN

History

Mobile Telephone Networks, more widely known as MTN, launched operations in 1994. With roots in South Africa, the company operates in 24 countries in Africa, Asia and Europe where it not only provides voice, data and digital services to retail customers, but also offers enterprise solutions to large corporates, small and medium enterprises, and government institutions.

Footprint

In Africa, MTN is present in Benin, Botswana, Cameroon, Congo Brazzaville, Côte d'Ivoire, Ghana, Guinea Bissau, Guinea, Kenya, Liberia, Namibia, Nigeria, Rwanda, South Africa, Sudan, South Sudan, Swaziland, Uganda and Zambia. In Asia, MTN is present in Iran, Syria, Yemen, and Afghanistan. In Europe, it is present in Cyprus.

From its roots in Africa, and with a vision to "lead the delivery of a bold, new digital world to our customers", MTN has become

---

37 Kenyans top Africa in smartphone, internet use in by Collins Omulo in Daily Nation, March 4, 2019. Pg 3

a global telecommunications giant. This was attained with the spread and financial capacity from its operations in Africa.

Reach

MTN's footprint growth has moved in tandem with the rapid expansion of its subscribers on its network. In 2011, MTN launched a 4G LTE network. The following year, MTN achieved a major milestone by attaining 200 million subscribers on its network. The same year, it became the first African brand to be listed in the BrandZ Top 100 Most Valuable Global Brands. As at March 2018, MTN had a total subscriber base of over 221.3 million. This is in spite of regulatory mandates in Nigeria and Uganda, for MTN in both countries to comply with subscriber registration stipulations and disconnect 10.4 million and 6.7 million subscribers respectively. MTN also employs over 21,000 staff of 59 different nationalities, and has the largest market share in 15 countries. In almost 70% of the countries where it operates, the company continues to grow. In 2015, in spite of challenges in its several operating entities, MTN commissioned 3,116 2G sites, 789 co-located 3G sites and 5,241 co-located LTE sites as well as 1,469 kilometres of long-distance fibre cable to enhance its voice and data network.

Financial Performance

MTN has also diversified its revenue streams, growing non-voice revenue to over 30% of its total annual revenues in 2015.

Revenue Streams

- Outgoing voice – 58%
- Data – 23%

- Incoming voice – 10%
- Devices – 5%
- SMS – 3%
- Other – 1%

It is useful to note that while outgoing voice revenue declined by 5%, data traffic increased by 108.5%, with concomitant growth in data revenue by 32.6%. Significantly, Nigeria has become the largest market for MTN, contributing more than 67 million subscribers, as at December 2018, according to the Nigerian Communications Commission (NCC). Together, Nigeria and South Africa contribute 63% of MTN's total revenues.

MTN also serves over 22.7 million Mobile Money customers in 15 markets,[38] and this is now an increasing contributor to the revenues of some MTN country operations, from 6% in Ghana and Rwanda, and reaching 17% in Uganda. Its Mobile Money product facilitates international remittances, savings, lending and insurance for MTN's customers across its network. MTN also announced its intention to acquire a payment service banking licence in Nigeria that would enable it offer mobile money services.[39] These moves reaffirm MTN's stated intention to be the largest bank in Africa.

---

38 For a comprehensive status update on MTN operations in Africa, see http//www. mtn.com.

39 MTN to acquire banking licence in Nigeria, say CEO on The Cable. November 13, 2018 in www.thecable.ng/just-in-mtn-to-acquire-banking-in-nigeria-says-ceo

Chapter Six

OPENING THE SKIES IN AFRICA

Aviation and air travel within African has grown over the years. Aviation in Africa effectively commenced in 1910, with a flight from Johannesburg to Cape Town. After over a century, this growth trajectory in air travel in Africa has continued. In an *Air Passenger Market Analysis* report, the International Air Transport Association (IATA) states that while global air passenger traffic recorded a 9.5% growth in passenger kilometres from March 2017 to March 2018, Africa-based airlines recorded a growth of 11.2% in international passenger traffic during the same period, with the routes between Africa and Europe, and Africa and Asia showing strong performance. The improved economic performance and increased business confidence in Nigeria and South Africa are important strong growth drivers.[40]

---

40 Air passenger growth completes a strong first quarter of 2018, Passenger Market Analysis in *iata.org/publications/economics/Report*.

Challenges remain, though. Since 1960, about 397 airlines in Africa have collapsed.[41] Nonetheless, the continent is now essentially air-covered. All the 55 African countries have international airports, with regular or periodic flights into and out of the countries. This has also progressed in tandem with the development of aviation infrastructure, consisting of airports, hangars, training facilities, and the promotion and establishment of domestic, regional and international airlines emanating out of Africa. Interestingly, the airlines with the widest coverage or ambition in Africa – *Ethiopian Airlines, Kenya Airways, South African Airways, Rwandair* – use and express *Africa* in their slogans or vision statements: *Kenya Airways* – The Pride of Africa; *Ethiopian Airlines* – The New Spirit of Africa; *South African Airways* – Africa's Leading World-Class Airline; *Rwandair* – Fly the dream of Africa.

This clearly means that Africa is the centrepiece of their vision.

Today there are over 200 airports and airstrips in Africa, with South Africa and Nigeria having the largest number. Well-known domestic, regional and international airlines in Africa include *Ethiopian, Kenya Airways, South African Airways, EgyptAir, Royal Air Maroc, Air Mauritius, ASKY, RwandAir, Air Côte D'Ivoire, Air Burkina, Precision Air* and many more. For our purposes here, we will focus on *Ethiopian*, as it is one of the largest and most successful airlines in Africa.

It is important to state that despite improvements, flying within Africa remains severely fraught with difficulties, delays and the frequent absence of connecting flights to cities and regions within the continent. Passengers are compelled to wait at

---

41 Open skies would lead to growth of Africa's airlines by Moses K. Gahigi in The East Africa March 2- 8, 2019 pg 36.

airports for long hours to connect to nearby cities and countries. Flights from Lagos to Monrovia, Freetown or Conakry could take three stops. Also, a flight from Lagos to Douala that should normally last one hour, could entail two to three stops through Lomé, Cotonou or Abidjan – and with a flight time lasting six to nine hours. Nonetheless, this weak state of development provides a massive opportunity for governments and private-sector operators in Africa to develop aviation infrastructure specifically and transport infrastructure generally.

Single African Air Transport Market

The launch and signing of the Single African Air Transport Market (SAATM) on 28 January 2018, in Addis Ababa, Ethiopia, by 23 African countries is an exemplar of the integration of the aviation sector in Africa. The SAATM is an outcome of the AU's effort to "create a single unified air transport market in Africa, the liberalisation of civil aviation in Africa and an impetus to the continent's economic integration agenda".[42] This is a critical initiative of the AU's 2063 Agenda. In furtherance of the implementation of the open skies initiative under the Yamoussoukro Decision of 1999 and the SAATM, the Ministerial Working Group met in Lomé, Togo, in May 2018, and signed a memorandum of implementation to activate the initiatives. Qualifying African airlines can formally seek to fly routes in other African countries without necessarily returning to their home country airports. The host, President Faure Gnassingbé of Togo, was also pleased that the African Development Bank (AfDB) committed to support the SAATM and the Yamoussoukro Decision. Nonetheless, the initiative

---

42 https.//au.int/en/newsevents/201801www.

is still a work in progress, as it was tested in December 2018. The Kenya Civil Aviation Authority (KCAA) declined granting *Ethiopian Airlines* (ET) a licence to operate scheduled passenger flight services on the Johannesburg-Nairobi–Brussels route, which would have meant *Ethiopian* flying directly to Brussels from Nairobi. In the same vein, *Kenya Airways* faulted *Ethiopian* for protectionism, stating that *"Ethiopian Airlines* do not allow more operators into their country."[43]

Support for the initiatives also came from New Partnership for African Development, Regional Economic Communities (REC) and the World Bank.[44]

Tourism

Tourism in Africa has witnessed consistent growth. International arrivals into the continent in 2017, grew to about 62 million – a growth rate of 8%.[45] Intra-African tourism, therefore, represents a great opportunity and enormous potential in boosting intra-African commerce, industry and integration. Mauritius, Rwanda, Kenya, Nigeria, Ghana and Ethiopia allow the issuance of visa on arrival for different categories of visiting Africans. Mozambique and Kenya have also signed an agreement allowing for visa-free travels by citizens of both

---

43 https://www.businessdailyafrica.com/news/Nairobi-says-no-to-ET-extra-route-request/539546-4878636-7jyseiz/index.html, and https://www.the-star.co.ke/news/2018/12/11/ethiopian-airlines-frustrating-open-skies-deal-mikosz_c1863875

44 *President Gnassingbé, African Ministers, experts push frontiers* on SAATM By Roland Ohaeri & Kayode Oyero in https://aviationbusinessjournal.aero/2018/06/11/president-gnassingbe-african-ministers-experts-push-frontiers-on-saatm/.

45 *http://media.unwto.org/press-release/2018-01-15/2017-international-tourism-results-highest-seven-years.*

countries.[46] Many other countries will, over time, adopt this measure and allow ease of entry into their territories. With greater ease of movement, the intra-African tourist or business executive or plain traveller will feel unrestricted to explore and discover the sights and sounds of the continent, spend on, and potentially engage in cross-border investments. The opportunities abound as intra-African travel continues to grow. In Rwanda where tourism grew by 23% between 2012 and 2016, there were 1,307,000 tourists who spent the night in Rwanda in 2016, out of which 84% were tourists from Africa.[47] In the same vein Kenya has invested in developing the tourism markets of Nigeria, Ethiopia, Uganda, South Africa and Rwanda. The Kenyan Tourism Board organised a two-day training workshop in June 2018 for travel agents. These efforts have contributed to a 46% growth in arrivals from Nigeria between 2009 and 2017.[48] In fact, though Kenya expected an increase of 17% to 18% in the number of tourist arrivals and incremental revenues of 15% from the 1.47 million tourists and the sum of $1.19 billion generated in 2017, there were two million international visitors in 2018, representing a growth of 37%, and generating revenues of KES157 billion or $1.57 billion, relative to the sum of KES119

46 Uhuru and Mozambican President Nyusi sign agreements :: Kenya https://www.standardmedia.co.ke/business/article/2001303541/kenya-and-mozambique-abolish-visa-rule

47 "Offside! Is Rwanda sponsorship of Arsenal a flashy own goal?" By Lisa Delpy Neirotti in *The East African,* 16th-22nd June, 2018.

48 "Africa Accounts for 29pc of Kenya's international arrivals", by Annie Njanja in *Business Daily* Kenya on 11th June 2018.

billion or $1.19 billion generated in 2017.[49] These initiatives are happening when, in East Africa, both Uganda and Tanzania have initiated efforts to revive their national airlines. Deploying government and private-sector promotional activities, Tanzania grew tourist arrivals to 1.3 million in 2017, while associated foreign exchange earnings from tourism increased by 13.6% from $2.115 billion for the period ended June 2017; and from that to $2,403 billion for the period ended June 2018, according to the Central Bank. Also, Ethiopia, Rwanda and Uganda are working towards increasing the fleets of their national airlines – all in a bid to participate in the growing regional and pan-African tourism market.

The Flying *Ethiopian*

Ethiopian Airlines,[50] more popularly known as *Ethiopian*, is Africa's largest, longest-running and most profitable airline. It launched its operations in April 1946 and has maintained uninterrupted operations for over 70 years. From its first scheduled flight on 8 April 1946 to Cairo through Asmara, deploying a Douglas C-47 Skytrain, *Ethiopian* now has over 100 international and 21 domestic routes, with 51 in Africa, 25 in the Middle East and Asia,

49 Earnings from tourism to hit Sh120bn this year, says Balala in https://www.businessdailyafrica.com/economy/3946234-4791740-m1wsoi/index.html OCTOBER 4, 2018. ; https://www.standardmedia.co.ke/business/article/2001308764/ investors-toast-to-tourism-earnings. Investors toast to tourism earnings. The Standard January 9, 2010. P.35; https://www.thecitizen.co.tz/News/Tourism-earnings-climb-13-6pc--BoT-report-shows/1840340-4747694-l200hgz/index.html. Tanzania secures is second Airbus, eyes international routes. The East African. January 12-18, 2019. Pp 5; Rwandair expansion on course as it signs deal for direct flights to Israel. The East African. January 12-18, 2019. Pp 5; Museveni pushes team to launch Uganda Airlines. The East African. January 12-18, 2019. Pp 4
50 For a report on the history, profile, status and strategy of *Ethiopian* Airlines see, www.flyethiopian.com. Information in this chapter is drawn largely from the site.

and 17 in Europe and America. In a highly-challenged industry, where bankruptcy has laid waste to many promising airlines, *Ethiopian* has become a dependable partner in the movement of people and goods within and outside Africa and an ever-present feature in the African skyline. It is expected that the airline will recover from the unfortunate air crash of its Boeing 737 Max 8 jet flight ET 302 from Addis Ababa to Nairobi at Bishoftu, in Ethiopia in March 2019. It is also profitable, proving that the airline business is still a viable business. *Ethiopian* has set itself to be a modern and technology-driven airline, operating the youngest and most modern fleet in Africa. The airline has a total operating fleet of 100 aircraft and 68 aircraft on order. With over 12,600 employees as at January 2017, *Ethiopian* espouses a vision "to become the most competitive and leading aviation group in Africa by providing safe, market-driven and customer-focused passenger and cargo transport, aviation training, flight catering, MRO and ground services by 2025".

Ethiopian operates from its hub at the Bole International Airport in Addis Ababa.[51] Located just eight kilometres from the city centre, it is one of the largest airports in Africa, processing 6.5 million passengers and 350,000 tons of cargo annually. The airport has been at the centre of the airline's evolution and growth and has played the role of a regional and continental hub for decades, serving as a distributive conduit for passengers and cargo coming from and leaving different parts of Africa to Asia, Europe, the Americas and other parts of the world.

---

51 www.addisairport.com

Pioneering Operations

The airline has pioneered many initiatives in the development of the airline industry in Africa. It has led the acquisition of many modern aircrafts in Africa. In 1961, it launched the first direct air service by any airline between East and West Africa with the commencement of the Addis Ababa and Monrovia flight through Khartoum, Sudan and Accra, Ghana.

It also set up a Cargo Management Department to develop the airline's cargo services as a business in 1989. On 1 June 1984, *Ethiopian* set a global record in distance flown by a commercial twin-engine jet after a thirteen-and-a-half-hour delivery flight from New York when its first Boeing 767 landed at the Addis Airport. In addition, the airline announced in 2005 its choice as Boeing's new Dreamliner's 787 launch carrier, as it placed an order for ten jets, with an option for five more, at a cost of $1.3 billion. This pledge was fulfilled when the Dreamliner arrived Addis Airport on 11 December 2011. The following year, on 19 September 2012, it became the first African airline to receive the Boeing 777 Freighter. In 2009, it placed an order for 35 new aircrafts and 20 units of 737 MAX 8s from Boeing. This was the largest single order of aircrafts by any airline in Africa.

Maintenance Capabilities

The airline also has a state-of-the-art hangar and maintenance base in Addis Ababa with the capacity to undertake airframe maintenance, D-checks, engine overhaul, components modification, repair and overhaul, light aircraft maintenance, avionics and technical work, not only for *Ethiopian*, but also for other airlines. In fact, *Ethiopian's* MRO capability for shop overhaul for CFM56-3 engines, etc., has received approval from the Ethiopian Civil Aviation Authority (ECAA) and the US Federal Aviation Administration (FAA). To strengthen its technological capacity, it opened a modern and purpose-built jet engine test facility which facilitates the ground testing of aircraft engines with a thrust of up to 45,000 kg (100,000lbs). It continued on this path and constructed a new maintenance hangar and cargo terminal complexes in 2006.

Code Sharing

To expand its network and facilitate connectivity for its passengers, *Ethiopian* has entered into code share agreements with 26 international airlines, including *Lufthansa, Brussels Airlines, Turkish, South African, ASKY, Egyptair, TAP Portugal, Singapore Airlines, Asiana Airlines, Air India, ANA, United Airlines, Austrian Airlines, Scandinavian Airlines,* offering its passengers connecting options from its hub in Addis Ababa to other parts of the world. In 2011, it joined the Star Alliance, a global airline network started in 1997 by five airlines – *Air Canada, Lufthansa, United, Scandinavian* and *THAI* – which now own a network of 27 airlines.

Building Capacity

As a measure to make the airline regenerating and self-sustainable, *Ethiopian* set up the Ethiopian Aviation Academy with a renewed vision to "be the most competitive and leading aviation training centre in Africa by 2025", and with a mission to "become the leading Aviation Academy in Africa by providing competitive global standard aviation training services".

The Academy was certified by the International Civil Aviation

Organisation as the ICAO Regional Training Centre of Excellence in May 2016. It was also accorded the European Aviation Safety Agency (EASA) Part-147 type maintenance training organisation certification and the MRO Unit secured EASA's approval. The Academy was, in 2018, ranked one of the top aviation training centres in the world by *Aviation Voice*, a leading global news medium. It offers capacity building in different fields such as:

1. Pilot Training

The Pilot Training School, set up in 1964, offers commercial licence training for pilots, including instrument and multi-engine rating (CPL/IR/ME) as well as multi-crew pilot licence and simulator. The training school meets all *Ethiopian's* requirements for pilots. Significantly, it has also trained pilots from 52 countries in Africa, Asia, Europe and the Middle East. Its pilot licensing programmes are accredited by ICAO, AFCAC, AFRAA, and ECAA.

2. Maintenance Training

The Aircraft Maintenance Technician School was set up in 1967, offering basic-type and recurrent theoretical and practical training. It provides competent technicians to *Ethiopian* and other regional airlines, on Boeing, Bombardier, MD11 and other aircraft types. It is accredited by ECAA, FAA and EASA.

3. Cabin Crew Training

The training centre has been in existence for more than 57 years and offers professional theoretical and practical training to cabin crew members.

4. Commercial and Ground Services

It provides basic theoretical and practical training in conformity with national and international regulations, with a focus on customer service, sales and ground services.

5. Leadership and Career Development

These programmes started in 1968 and comprises leadership and career development programmes in corporate governance, decision-making and problem solving, transformational leadership, project management, financial management, etc. Employees are also challenged with opportunities and responsibilities. In 1957, Alemayehu Abebe, the first Ethiopian commercial aircraft commander, captained the DC-3/47 aircraft on a solo flight. Also in 1971, the airline made Colonel Semret Medhane the first Ethiopian General Manager of the airline.

6. Diversity in Action

To promote "Women Empowerment for a Sustainable Growth", *Ethiopian* operated an all-women functioned flight, from Addis Ababa to Bangkok on 19 November 2015. Women were the flight deck crew members; they took charge of airport operations, flight planning, flight operations, cabin operations, ramp operations, baggage handling, cargo handling, on-board logistics, and everything else that had to be done.

Furthermore, in December 2016, *Ethiopian* operated its first all-female crew in a domestic flight within Africa. The Boeing 777 flight from Addis Ababa, Ethiopia, to Lagos, Nigeria, consisted of pilots, cabin crew, check-in staff and its ground flight dispatchers who were all women.[52]

Financial Performance

Ethiopian is well run and is the most profitable airline in Africa. In 2016, the airline increased its revenues, by 8.6%, to $2.3 billion, arising from business growth in flight frequency and an expansion in its routes, with a corresponding increase in profitability to $261.9 million from $150.9 million in 2015. It has an interesting passenger carriage model. In the same year it flew 7.6 million passengers, out of which 75% were transit passengers. Significantly, it grew the number of passengers carried by 20% during the period.[53] In the 2017/2018 fiscal year the pattern of strong financial performance continued, as *Ethiopian* grew in its key parameters. The total number of passengers carried during the period grew by 21% to 10.6 million. Its total revenues increased by 43% to $3.21 billion, and profitability inched up $233 million from $229 million while the airline added 14 aircrafts to its fleet, as well as 21 new destinations during the fiscal year.[54]

Recognition and Awards

Ethiopian has won numerous international awards. In 2015 alone, it won 21 different awards. President Barack Obama

---

52 Helen Cooffey. 20th December 2017. www.independent.co.uk *Ethiopian Airlines* Operates First All-Female Flight Crew in Africa.

53 *Ethiopian* carrier flies high, doubling profits, by Allan Olingo in *East African*, 6th September 2017; *Ethiopian Airlines Annual Report* 2015/2016 in https://www.ethiopianairlines.com.

54 "Sell Ethiopian Airlines minority stake to African governments, CEO urges" by *Andualem Sisay* in *The East African*, 10th August 2018.

visited *Ethiopian Airlines* during his three-day official visit to Ethiopia in July 2015. Also, Ban Ki-Moon, UN Secretary-General nominated *Ethiopian's* CEO Mr Tewolde GebreMariam to his High-Level Advisory Group on Sustainable Transport.

Impact of Intra-African Trade and Integration

While *Ethiopian Airlines* has proven to be a successful African Torchbearer airline, its role and impact as a facilitator of trade and commerce has not received as much attention. In exploring this nexus, I have focused on *Ethiopian's* intra-African aviation through its partnership and alliances with other country and regional airlines in the continent, and its participation in intra-African and international commerce through its freight and cargo activities.

Intra-African Aviation Initiatives

In 2009 *Ethiopian* Airlines signed a management agreement with ASKY, a regional airline with its hub in Lomé, Togo. This has opened the two airlines to cooperation and expanded operations to West and Central Africa and other parts of the world. *Ethiopian* owns 40% shareholding in ASKY and Lomé became its second hub in 2012. In 2013, it signed two significant agreements. First, it became the strategic partner of *Malawian Air*, with 49% shareholding. Second, it signed an MOU with the Djibouti International Airport to provide cargo transportation of goods in East Africa. *Ethiopian Airlines* also has an agreement with Zambia Airways. In its search for dominance of the African skyline, and as part of its Vision 2025 business strategy, *Ethiopian* has entered into joint venture agreements and understanding with no less than 14 countries in Africa. The countries include Tchad, Djibouti, Equatorial Guinea, Guinea, Malawi, Zambia, Mozambique, DRC, Togo, in addition to its existing business activities with Air Côte d'Ivoire.[55]

In fact, the government of Tchad and *Ethiopian* announced an agreement to launch a new airline – "Tchadia Airlines" – in which it will own 51% and *Ethiopian* will own 49%.[56] The inaugural flight took off on 1 October 2018. Quite critical is the confidence that the governments have in *Ethiopian*'s capacity to run country airlines with high standards in their countries.

How Aviation Facilitates Intra–African Commerce and industry

Beyond its leading position in air passenger traffic in Africa, *Ethiopian* has also emerged as the leading air freight airline in the continent, indicating its direct role as a harbinger and facilitator of intra-African commerce and industry. Just as global air freight grew by 31.6%, and an associated growth in capacity by 7.6%, by June 2017, African airlines recorded the fastest growth in cargo volumes in seven years, facilitated by the growing trade between Africa and Asia, particularly China, whose trade with Africa grew by almost 60% in six months up to June 2017. *Ethiopian* has positioned itself even further for these emergent international and regional trade opportunities, with its CEO stating that "we are building one of the world's largest cargo terminals, and having new-generation and high-performance

55 Ethiopian Airlines poised to take over Africa skies in *The East African* 19th August 2018 in http://www.theeastafrican.co.ke.

56 "Tchad signs deal with Ethiopian Airlines to launch carrier." 4th September 2018 in https://www.standardmedia.co.ke/business/article/Tchad-signs-deal-with -ethiopian-airlines-to-launch-carrier.

aircrafts shows our commitment in supporting the continent's growing cargo and logistics services." The airline reached an agreement with Boeing to acquire four air freighters, including two Boeing 777s which cost $651.4 million. Overall, the airline ordered ten Airbus A350-900 planes costing over $3 billion.[57]

With these investments and its innovativeness in being the African airline that pioneered the highly advanced freight carrier, the B777-200LR freighter, it was not surprising that *Ethiopian* won the African Cargo Airline of the Year award in 2017, operating 30 destinations in Africa, the Middle East, Asia and Europe using six B777 and two B757 freighters. Its major cargo destinations are Belgium (Brussels & Liege), Hong Kong, Shanghai, Bombay, New Delhi, Dubai, South Africa, Lomé and Lagos.[58]

In the same vein, in July 2018, it was reported that Ethiopian Cargo and DHL, the global trade and logistics giant, had reached an understanding to establish a joint venture company, with Ethiopian Cargo owning 51% and DHL owing 49%.[59]

These initiatives clearly mark *Ethiopian* as a forward-looking airline that is building a viable and sustainable domestic and international airline business, contributing directly to intra-African trade, facilitating the movement of people in Africa and the integration of African industry and commerce.

---

57 "African airlines fly high with cargo on the back of a strong economy" by Allan Olingo in *The East African,* August 14, 2017.

58 "SAA Cargo loses top spot as African cargo carrier to Ethiopian Airlines." 2016-04-29 12:00 - Louzel Lombard in https://www.traveller24.com/News/Flights/saa-cargo-loses-top-spot-as-african-cargo-carrier-to-ethiopian-airlines-20160429

59 "Reports link Ethiopian and DHL in joint venture." 09 / 07 / 2018 in http://www.aircargonews.net/news/airline/freighter-operator/single-view/news

PART III

FINANCING AFRICA

Chapter Seven

INTEGRATING FINANCIAL
SERVICES IN AFRICA*

A defining objective of the African Union is to *promote sustainable development at the economic, social and cultural levels as well as the integration of African economies.* This noble mandate, enshrined in Article 3 of the Constitutive Acts of the AU, actually predates the AU, and was a principal goal of the Organisation of African Unity, OAU, the predecessor body of the AU.

Economic integration also provided a fundamental impetus in the formation of the various Regional Economic Communities (RECs) and monetary zones in Africa such as ECOWAS, UEMOA, CEMAC, CEEAC, EAC, AMU, CEN-SAD, SADC, COMESA, IGAD, etc. Together, these RECs have striven to promote and coordinate social, political and economic integration in the continent. Interestingly, some countries are even members of up to two or three RECs. This is a testament to the overarching criticality of economic integration in the vision, plans and activities of African states.

In this chapter I will focus on the integration of financial services in Africa, a field, though unheralded, where remarkable results are being recorded. A payment system, for instance, is a facilitator of monetary transactions and a veritable integrative node. In the UEMOA zone in West Africa, the *Groupement Interbancaire Monétique de l'Union Economique et Monétaire Ouest Africaine (*more widely known by its French acronym GIM-UEMOA) was set up by BCEAO, the Central Bank of West African States in 2003, to create a cashless region. It has grown to become a regional platform for cards, electronic payments and clearing of interbank transactions. With over 100 banks, financial and postal institutions as members, cardholders in the GIM network pay relatively low transaction fees.

Also, the Central African equivalent, GIMAC, created in 2013 under the guidance of the Central Bank of Central African States (BEAC), is working with banks to integrate the electronic payment system in the region and ensure inter-operability and acceptance of GIMAC cards for ATMs, POS, etc., for international payments. This will reduce transaction and cash handling costs while facilitating e-commerce.

The East African Payment System (EAPS) provides a platform for the real-time settlement of cross-border payments in the region. Driven by the central banks in the region, and piloted in 2013, the payment system took off immediately in Kenya, Uganda, Tanzania and, subsequently, Rwanda. More remarkable is that EAPS is based on direct convertibility and the use of the currencies of participating countries for transactions and settlement without the intermediary facilitation of any OECD currency. For instance, transactions initiated in Tanzania shillings can be directly settled in Uganda shillings or Kenya shillings.

In Southern Africa, the SADC Integrated Regional Electronic Settlement System (SIRESS) and the Regional Payment and Settlement System (REPSS), launched separately in 2014, are two integrative payments systems worth referencing. Through SIRESS, funds can be wired real time to beneficiaries with accounts in SIRESS commercial banks. REPSS, with a clearing house in Zimbabwe and the Central Bank of Mauritius as its settlement bank, utilises an electronic platform for cross-border payments and settlement.

Quite positively, these initiatives, operationalised under the auspices of central banks, and with the active participation of commercial banks, are technologically advanced, rapid and secure. While leveraging on the real-time gross settlement systems of the countries, they seek to enhance efficiency, reduce settlement time, lower transaction costs and generally facilitate intra-African trade and economic integration in the continent.

In line with these developments, the banking sector in Africa has, in the last decade, expanded exponentially in asset size and profitability; geography-distribution channels and network; product sophistication (digital banking, cards, mobile payments, etc.); and financial inclusion. In addition, access to financial services continues to improve across the continent. Furthermore, leveraging on enhanced capacity, pan-African banks are increasingly able to collaboratively finance large ticket and transformational infrastructural projects through syndications and risk sharing.

Beyond banking, we are also witnesses to the birth and growth of pan-African insurance, microfinance and other financial service companies across the continent that offer great diversity and depth of products and solutions. All these have led to the increase in the range and frequency of the classes of risks that banks and other financial institutions face. Concomitantly, risk management, regulatory compliance and corporate governance have become more stringent with onerous application, as they remain important variables for assessing the health of banks in the drive towards overall sector viability and sustainability.

Imperceptibly, but surely, the regulatory environment of the financial services sector is also being integrated. The Association of African Central Banks (AACB), headquartered in Dakar, brings together 39 regional and country central banks in Africa. In line with its statutes and practices, its Assembly of Governors usually meets yearly to deliberate on financial system stability, monetary and payment system integration, the African Central Bank initiative, etc. Another critical arm is the Community of African Banking Supervisors (CABS) which works to strengthen banking regulatory and supervisory frameworks. In the last decade, I have observed first-hand this increased collaboration between African central banks, with MOUs being signed to facilitate cross-border supervision, exchange of ideas and information sharing between host and home regulators. Also, the College of Supervisors set up by the Central Bank of Nigeria as a forum that brings together host regulators of banks to strengthen governance practices and ensure soundness in the banking sector, is also a positive development.

An evolving trend in the African banking space is the initiative to connect Africa and enable customers of a bank to conveniently access their accounts, deposit cash and make cheque withdrawals in any branch in different countries across Africa where the bank operates – outside the primary country holding the account. This has the distinct capability to alter the face and operation of banking in the continent as it will open up and facilitate easy movement of goods, services, capital and people. I also look forward to the day when a Moroccan manufacturer of fertiliser, visiting Zambia to negotiate a contract, agrees to payment terms, issues a payment instrument to a Zambian exporter of high-quality packaging materials and gets value immediately, using simple electronic payment instruments.

On the whole, these emerging trends contribute significantly to the ongoing Africa-led processes of creating a powerful, vibrant pan-African financial infrastructure to further undergird and deepen pan-African economic, commercial, business and social interactions through access to personal and business finance across Africa. Together with the various similar initiatives in different spheres by African economic communities identified above, these initiatives will serve as a powerful signal of the march of African economic advancement through financial facilitation, to build a fully integrated financial system that enhances financial inclusion and serves the people.

However, a lot of work remains to be done. To accelerate financial integration, existing regional mechanisms and frameworks, including those highlighted above, must now begin to coalesce and fuse into larger and functional pan-African financial systems, including strong and effective sub-regional central banks, common currency, payments and collections platforms, and other integrative structures to facilitate intra-African industry and trade, etc. Furthermore, given the importance of finance to agriculture, infrastructure, industry and economic development, the largest economies in each sub-region of the continent, in spite of their existing differences, should emerge and serve as regional anchors to drive integration within the defined framework of the Assembly of the African Union.

★ This chapter has been previously published as an article online.

Chapter Eight

BANKING AFRICA –
UNITED BANK FOR AFRICA (UBA)

It is difficult to write a story in which you are personally involved. My first formal encounter with United Bank for Africa (UBA) was in 1990 during my National Youth Service Corps (NYSC) programme. The scheme is a compulsory national programme in which Nigerian graduates from universities and polytechnics, who are below 30 years old, are required to serve the nation. To make it truly national and ensure diversity, "corpers" as they are called, are usually deployed to states other than their states of origin. The scheme is designed to promote national unity and nation building. The scheme also has a community development service where corpers work in, and support, the community they are serving in. The scheme consists of two parts. The first part is a three-week endurance and fitness bootcamp, called "camp" by the corps members. It consists of early morning aerobics and other physical exercises, rock climbing, patriotism training, language training, etc. It is one month of labour, work, sports, bonding and fun. The second part is an eleven-month work programme where corp members are deployed to work in government ministries, departments, agencies, educational institutions, health facilities, non-governmental organisations, private-sector companies, etc.

After the camp, I was required to open an account to receive my monthly NYSC allowance. My account was a UBA account.

UBA is a rare case in which the name of a firm becomes the mandate of the firm. When the founders of UBA conceived the Bank in 1949, as British and French Bank (BFB), the Nigerian subsidiary of the French Bank, they would never have thought that the leaders of the bank would, in 2007 – almost half a century later – commence the execution of the vision in the name, United Bank for Africa, to extend the bank's operations to over 600 locations in 20 African countries in West, Central, East and Southern Africa, with over 10 million customers – making it a leading bank and brand in Africa. In February 1961, the name United Bank for Africa was incorporated to take over the assets and liabilities of the BFB.

Origins

Trailing the origins of UBA is akin to the excavations of an archeologist or the expeditions of an explorer. A discovery generates excitement, interest and a curious search for more. A peel of one layer leads to other layers. It is endless.

The first peeled layer dates the origins of the bank to 1848, with the creation of Comptoir National d'Escompte de Mulhouse (CEM), created by manufacturers in engineering and textiles in the Alsace Region in Eastern France. The bank was focused on expansion through organic growth and acquisition. It continued to grow in operations, locations, sectors and industries until 1913 when the bank was broken into two separate banks – CEM, the parent bank, and a new independent subsidiary, the Banque Nationale de Credit (BNC) – bringing together the French branches.[60]

A second peeled layer trails the roots of the bank to 1932 when the Banque Nationale de Credit et Industries was created as an offshoot, to inherit the head office premises, employees and customers of BNC.

The bank was dynamic and also focused on expansion by organic growth and acquisitions. In addition to its large in-country network, it had 30 foreign subsidiaries and was the lead bank with foreign network operations in France. BNCI was innovative; it was the first bank in France to advertise on radio in 1954.

As World War II wore down European economies, and as colonialism lost its luster and the colonies moved inexorably towards independence, BNCI implemented a policy of converting its foreign branches to subsidiary entities.[61]

The third peeled layer, and the story which is more often told by the bank, takes off with the London branch of BNCI and BFB, which became an incorporated subsidiary and thereafter began to chart its own international business and expansion path. In 1949 the Nigerian branch of British and French Bank

---

60   https://history.bnpparibas/document/cem-a-bank-with-its-roots-in-the-textile-and-engineering-industries/.

61   https://history.bnpparibas/document/an-innovative-bank-banque-nationale-pour-le-commerce-et-lindustrie-bnci/.

for Commerce and Industry was created in Lagos, Nigeria as the third foreign bank in Nigeria.

It is useful to note that the primary focus of these banks was to facilitate colonial commerce between Nigeria and the United Kingdom, and Europe in general.[62]

The fourth peeled layer references the incorporation and use of the name United Bank for Africa on 23 February 1961 when it inherited and took over the operations of the British and French Bank. It commenced full operations under its new name in October 1961. Like its pioneering forebearers, UBA was the first Nigerian bank to issue its shares for purchase by the investing public through an Initial Public Offer in 1970. UBA New York was opened in 1984 as the first bank in sub-Saharan Africa – outside South Africa – to commence operations in the US and North America.[63] UBA was also the first Nigerian bank to have a female chairperson – Bola Kuforiji-Olubi.

The fifth peeled layer of UBA occurred in August 2005 when UBA merged with Standard Trust Bank. The post-merger UBA is the new UBA.

Nigerian Industry Behemoth

During and after the merger of UBA and STB in August 2005, UBA began a rigorous process of institutional redefinition, with a review and presentation of its vision, mission and the raison d'être of the bank. It became evident that UBA desired to become an industry behemoth.

---

62 For additional information on the evolution, growth, and expansion of United Bank for Africa, see www.ubagroup.com.

63 Ibid

Working with Mckinsey, the consulting firm, UBA articulated a "three-tier strategic intent" which it defined as follows:

- dominance in the Nigerian banking industry
- leading bank in Africa
- presence in global money centres.

Actually, a prescient pledge to be an industry behemoth commenced earlier in June 1998 with a public declaration to the Nigerian Money Market Association by Tony Elumelu (CEO of the then Standard Trust Bank) when he posited that "it is our belief that in five years' time, the industry will begin to consolidate and large foreign institutions will start taking steps towards penetrating the Nigerian market. Our objective is to ensure that we build an institution that can play a leading role in that consolidation process".[64]

The merger with UBA, the third largest bank, was a declaration of intent for industry dominance in Nigeria, and its selective global presence was in line with the bank's strategic aspirations.

This focus on being a Nigerian banking industry behemoth manifested in an aggressive pursuit of network size and balance sheet size. For UBA at that time, size was everything. UBA became the largest bank in Nigeria, with over 500 branches. The *largest bank* accomplishment was loudly and proudly proclaimed on billboards and other media.

Relatedly, UBA became the biggest bank when it became the first bank to attain the ₦1 trillion in balance sheet size and

---

64   TOE: An Epitome of Humility by Udochi Nwaodu in *The Power of Vision – Insights on Tony Elumelu* – Tony Elumelu Foundation, 2010.

contingents in 2006. It was ranked the industry leader in Nigeria in 2007 by Agusto & Co.[65]

In 2006 Tony Elumelu, the Group CEO, called a meeting of the bank's seniors to share his vision for UBA to be the largest bank in Nigeria and to be the first bank to hit the ₦1 trillion asset base at the end of the financial year. He made a strong case for UBA to lead the Nigerian banking industry. The challenging and surprising part was that this session took place about four months to the end of the financial year, which was then 31 July 2006. It was a radical responsibility. It meant growing the balance sheet significantly and rapidly. But it was done. At the end of the financial year, having become the first bank in Nigeria to attain the ₦1 trillion asset base, UBA achieved its goal of dominating the Nigerian banking industry.

UBA continued with this expansionist strategy in Nigeria with a Public Offer and a Rights Issue in 2007. Using the Central Bank's window of Purchase and Assumption, UBA acquired the assets of the following banks that could not meet the new minimum capital requirement: City Express Bank, African Express Bank and Metropolitan Bank. UBA also became a leader in the industry's distribution network, with the largest number of accounts, branches and ATMs. This dominance focus also found expression in the comprehensive rebranding of the bank, its logo, internal and external communication, fascia, etc., in all its branches and head office.

---

65 www.ubagroup.com - Q1 2012 – Conference Call.

Leading African Bank

Once the decision had been taken to become a leading African bank, to expand operations into other African countries, UBA began a vociferous and methodological pursuit of this objective. Starting with Ghana, where the erstwhile Standard Trust Bank had commenced operations in January 2005, the initial focus was on a ring of coverage in West Africa. In Ghana, Standard Trust was the first Nigerian bank to be licensed in 2004 and was instrumental in changing the banking landscape to a more open and customer-oriented banking sector in the country. In a ceremony to commemorate the formal change of name from Standard Trust Ghana to UBA, Ghana's vice president, Alhaji Aliu Mahama, in January 2007, unveiled the new logo and encouraged the bank to support lending to micro and small-scale businesses, given their role in economic growth. The Central Bank governor, Paul Aquah, on the occasion, affirmed that the Central Bank will support the building of a "robust, diversified and globally competitive banking sector capable of meeting the developmental needs of the economy."[66]

Caffeinated Growth Strategy: 2008 – 2011

The period starting from January 2008, when UBA Cameroon commenced full operations in Douala, to July 2011, when UBA launched operations in Congo Brazzaville, was one of the fastest periods of expansion of international banking operations in the history of the banking industry in Africa, and perhaps the world. It was a very intense phase consisting of stakeholder engagements, meetings with central banks and

---

66 http://www.ghanaweb.com/GhanaHomePage/NewsArchive/Standard-Trust-Bank-is-now-UBA-11775Business News of Tuesday, 23 January 2007.

senior government officials, licensing, human and material resourcing, set-up of operations, launch of service to customers and growth of business.

Côte d'Ivoire and Cameroon were the initial launch pad hubs for the regional banking project. Like he did in Ghana, Tony Elumelu, then group CEO, led the Ivoirien bank licensing project, meeting with the minister of finance and local partners. Thereafter, the pan–African banking initiative was decentralised with Suzanne Iroche and, later, Rasheed Olaoluwa coordinating centrally; Fogan Sossah driving the expansion in the UEMOA, i.e., Francophone West Africa; Nnamdi Okonkwo coordinating the business in WAMZ, i.e. the West African Monetary Zone; Manz Denga shepherding in East Africa; and Emeke E. Iweriebor anchoring Central Africa – all as Regional CEOs. We also had responsibility to simultaneously drive country business operations in Côte d'Ivoire, Uganda and Cameroon respectively. This first phase of the African expansion programme had additional supportive roles by Jean-Luc Konan, Ellis Asu, Jacob Forbah, Rofur Mbunkur, Fon Ngando, Eyo Asuquo, Simeon Adigun, who worked with me on the programme, and several others, before it came to an end.

During the second facet, the focus moved to business consolidation and growth, and was aimed at deriving increased shareholder value from the operations of the country subsidiaries. I worked on this phase, at different times, with Kennedy Uzoka who subsequently became the group CEO of the Bank; Emmanuel Nnorom and Gabriel Edgal. Thereafter, the bank decentralised further, with the appointment of more executives focused on the African business, to accelerate the growth and deepen market share of the country businesses.

In addition to its strategy on greenfield licensing projects, the new UBA had explored brownfield acquisition opportunities in different parts of the continent. Ultimately, UBA, in 2009, acquired Banque Internationale du Burkina (BIB), the leading Bank in Burkina Faso, and Continental Banque du Benin (CBB) – also a leading Bank in Benin Republic. The expectation was that these brownfield banks would facilitate development of the UBA franchise for further expansion and business growth.

In line with this vision, UBA also activated the three-tier strategic intent. Though UBA had had a branch in New York since 1984, this phase required establishing presence in key international markets. UBA therefore initiated and finalised the acquisition of Afrinvest UK, a boutique investment banking firm, in 2007. This was then converted to UBA Capital UK to support the investment banking and international trade business of UBA Group. It operated from London. The plan was for UBA Capital UK to be the pathway for further expansion into other parts of Europe. In its continuing pursuit, UBA opened a representative office in Paris, France in March 2009,[67] to cater to its international customers doing business with France and other parts of Europe, and its growing expansion in Francophone Africa. At that time, UBA was operating in nine African countries, with five of them in Francophone Africa – Cameroon, Côte d'Ivoire, Benin, Burkina Faso and Senegal. UBA also faced the east. In 2007, UBA entered into an agreement with the China Development Bank to collaborate in the financing of infrastructural development projects across Africa. Along with Tony Elumelu, I participated in the Forum on China-Africa Cooperation (FOCAC) in Beijing in November

---

67 www.ubagroup.com.

2006. Prior to that, I had worked with a team from the China Development Bank on a Cooperation Agreement which was concretised in a landmark Memorandum of Understanding signed between both institutions. The Cooperation Agreement was based on a framework to support long-term infrastructural projects in Nigeria and other African countries. In our planning meetings preceding the signing ceremony, both in Lagos and Beijing, I realised that CDB was the largest developing financial institution in the world, and I was impressed by the sheer scale of the projects CDB had financed in China, including the Yangtze River Dam.

Chronology of Expansion

At the Q1 2012 Conference Call to investors,[68] UBA announced that with the launch of operations in DR Congo and Congo Republic, a key phase of expansion had been concluded. The emphasis would be on business consolidation and value extraction. Also, the ex-Nigeria business of the bank contributed 18% of the total revenues of the bank in 2011, a growth from 13% in 2010. The shares of the ex-Nigeria business of the bank continued to improve. At the nine-month 2013 Investor Conference Call, the bank announced that the African business contributed 22% of the total revenue of the Group. At the end of 2016, it had grown to 32%. By 2017, the African and non-Nigerian operations of UBA contributed 45% of the total earnings of the bank[69], making the vision of the bank to generate 50% of its revenues from outside Nigeria well within

---

68 www.ubagroup.com - Q1 2012 – Conference Call.
69 www.ubagroup.com - Q1 2012 – Conference Call

reach.[70] The bank's streak of winning awards began to steadily extend to Africa. UBA won the Best Transaction Bank in Africa award for 2014, awarded by *The Banker*. Same year, UBA won Best Emerging Market Bank of the Year in Cameroon, Senegal and Burkina Faso – all awarded by *Global Finance* magazine.

In 2016, UBA won the Best Bank Awards in Cameroon, Senegal, Tchad, Gabon and Congo. Also, in 2017, UBA won the Best Bank in Africa award. So, in addition to increasingly strong financial performance of its African subsidiaries, the work of building a pan-African institution was receiving recognition and validation locally and internationally.

New Face of Communication

To showcase its pan-African presence and global aspirations, UBA started to project soft power and aggressively showcase its credentials in many ways. UBA began to hire Africans and non-Africans who were deployed to important roles in UBA Group's operations. The bank also began to more actively advertise in international media. News releases from the bank were also translated into French and Portuguese and disseminated in many international news media, especially in the countries of presence.

There was the increased realisation of the benefits of leveraging on the media to cultivate a consistently positive image of the institution in order to facilitate business growth.

Another expression was the focus on digital and social media, content creation and management, and the need for these areas

---

70 Investor Presentation, May 2018. P.5. https://www.ubagroup.com/ir

to be adequately resourced. The bank created its own YouTube Channel, *RedTV*, with a name to match its dominant brand colour. The TV channel had both English and French content. It operated as a lifestyle channel with content consisting of fashion, food, music and dance, travel, etc. The target audience is the young and millennial segment of the population.

The focused and directed engagement of the media ensured the retention of existing and potential customers in Nigeria and across Africa.

Entwined Giving

UBA Foundation[71] is the defined corporate social responsibility outreach arm of UBA Group. The Foundation focuses on the "socio-economic betterment of the communities in which the bank operates", with a primary focus on environment, education, economic empowerment and special projects. These areas of focus nurtured goodwill for the bank and honoured its communities.

Environment

The Foundation identified and selected some large road intersections in its communities of operation that needed reconstruction. Thereafter, the location or environment is cleaned up, landscaped with beautiful plants and maintained. Though this initiative started in Nigeria, it has now been given a pan-African flavour with its extension to Tchad and other locations.

---

71 For additional information on the activities of UBA Foundation, see www. ubagroup.com.

Education

This area has received significant attention from UBA Foundation. This was expressed in many of the Foundation's programmes, including the donation of braille machines to a visually impaired high school student who participated in the Foundation's flagship National Essay Competition launched in 2011.

Other initiatives include the refurbishment of the labour ward of the University of Lagos Teaching Hospital and re-equipping the Cardiac Centre of the University of Benin.

The Foundation also built hostel accommodation for university students, ICT centres, provided training, scholarships, etc. Nonetheless, the flagship educational projects of the Foundation were the National Essay Competition and the Read Africa Project.

The National Essay Competition was a competition organised for high schools – initially in Nigeria, and subsequently, in Ghana, Senegal, Gabon, Mozambique and other countries. A topic is selected and students invited to write essays on the subject. The essays are then assessed by reputable university professors. A special commemoration programme is organised to select the winners of the competition. The winner carts away a full scholarship to a university in the country. Other winners also get computers and other educational materials. I supported the scheme, and in October 2015, gave the keynote speech at UBA's amphitheatre to a group of students from several high schools in Nigeria. I encouraged them to read and write, as this will create opportunities for them in their future endeavours.

The second flagship educational programme of the Foundation is the Read Africa Project which was launched in 2011. The initiative is aimed at awakening and enhancing interest in the committed study of educative books by providing relevant literary books to high school students in Africa, especially in light of the pervasive and growing influence of social media. Books given out by the UBA Foundation include *Weep Not, Child* by Ngũgĩ wa Thiong'o, *Purple Hibiscus* by Chimamanda Ngozi Adichie, *Fine Boys* by Eghosa Imasuen, and others. In November 2018, UBA Foundation launched a Community Day Service initiative entitled "Each One Teach One" across the bank's operational countries. It was focused on the staff of the bank directly contributing and giving back to society.[72]

---

72 UBA Launches Each One Teach One. November 30, 2018 https://www. standardmedia.co.ke/business/article/2001304648/uba-launches-each-one-teach-one-initiative

Chapter Nine

INSURING AFRICA

SAHAM

The SAHAM Group is an African conglomerate that started with insurance, but diversified into finance, health services, education, real estate, business process outsourcing, etc.

The group was founded in 1995 by Moulay Hafid Elalamy, a Moroccan entrepreneur. Prior to that, he was the CEO of the African Insurance Company of Morocco.[73] The group built its business on the five values of entrepreneurship: excellence, ethics, innovation and solidarity. After its set-up in 1995, SAHAM deployed a dual strategy of organic growth, strategic acquisitions and partnerships to scale up its operations. In 1996 it acquired AGMA and followed swiftly with Lahlou-Tazi in 1997. Both companies were merged, listed and then sold in 1998. This is indicative of an early inclination to boldness.

---

73 For a report on the history, profile, status, business and strategy of Saham Group see, www.sahamgroup.com

SAHAM kickstarted its diversification strategy in 1999 with the establishment of Phone Group, which set up customer relationship centres and later partnered with Bertelsmann, a leading communications firm in Europe, in 2004. Though acquisitions and mergers continued, SAHAM's major break in its expansionist drive got a major fillip in 2010 with the acquisition of 92% shareholding of Groupe Colina, a leading insurance company with presence in 17 African countries. Thereafter, it never really looked back, as it acquired Angola Seguros, the leader in the Angolan Insurance market with 16% market share, as well as 81% of Lebanese LIA Insurance from Audi Bank. This was the launchpad for expansion into North Africa and the Middle East. The aggressive trend continued. SAHAM went east with the acquisition of 66.7% of Mercantile Insurance of Kenya in 2013. In 2014 SAHAM Finances, the company, acquired 66% of CORAR AG Ltd, a large and leading Rwandan insurance company. As a measure of the growing significance of intra-African economic collaboration exemplified by SAHAM's investment in Rwanda, President Paul Kagame led a delegation from Rwanda to meet leading Moroccan business leaders in Casablanca on 21 June 2016, as part of a two-day trip to Morocco. He had earlier been decorated with Morocco's highest national award, the Grand Collar of Wissam Al-Mohammed by King Mohammed VI.[74] Also in 2014, SAHAM acquired UNITRUST Insurance of Nigeria. The SAHAM Group has built a large and diversified business with revenues in excess of $1.1 billion, with 9,500 employees, and is present in the following 27 countries:

- North Africa - Algeria, Morocco and Tunisia

---

74 www.KT .com

- West Africa - Benin, Burkina Faso, Côte d'Ivoire, Ghana, Mali, Niger, Nigeria, Togo and Senegal
- Central Africa and Southern Africa - Angola, Botswana, Cameroon, Gabon and Congo
- Middle East - Egypt, Lebanon and Saudi Arabia
- East Africa - Kenya, Rwanda, Madagascar and Mauritius
- Europe - France and Luxembourg.

Its real estate arm, SAHAM Immobilier, provides environment-friendly housing in Morocco while the group's Sana Education focuses on providing "a network of high-quality teaching establishments throughout Africa" and targets 100,000 students within a decade.[75]

In expression of its ambition to become a pan-African insurance group, and in a significant and strategic overhaul of the insurance sector in Africa, Sanlam Insurance, South Africa's largest insurance company announced, in 2018, its 100% acquisition of Saham Finances for $1 billion. This immediately created a gateway to Saham's north African and sub-saharan African businesses and 65 subsidiaries. It had commenced the process by initially acquiring 30% shareholding in 2016 and, thereafter, increasing its shareholding to 46.6% in 2017.[76]

NSIA

NSIA[77] is an African financial services group with origins in Côte d'Ivoire and interests primarily in insurance, and recently,

---

75 www.sahamgroup.com

76 Sanlam buys out Morocco's SAHAM Finances in $1 billion African expansion https://www.reuters.com/article/us-sanlam-semil-stake/sanlam-buys-out-moroccos-saham-finances-in-1-billion-african-expansion-idUSKCN1GK0LJ

77 For a report on the history, profile, status, business and strategy of NSIA, see www.nsiagroupe.com.

banking. It commenced operations in 1995. Its key objective is to lead in bancassurance products and services by 2017. NSIA operates in 12 countries.

The NSIA adventure began in 1995 with the creation of a general insurance company by Jean Kacou Diagou in Côte d'Ivoire. Prior to setting up NSIA in 1995, he had been the vice chairman of AXA Group in Africa, the large French multinational insurance firm, and was also part of the team that negotiated the harmonisation of insurance laws and statues, and the co-drafting of the code for Conference Interafricaine des Marches d'Assurance, more widely known as CIMA, in Francophone Africa.[78] The following year, in 1996, NSIA acquired the life and non-life business of AGF i.e., Assurances Generales de France.

The NSIA Group then began a process of organic and inorganic expansion, growing internally and acquiring entities across Africa. Twenty years later, NSIA operates in 12 countries of Central and West Africa: Benin, Cameroon, Congo, Côte d'Ivoire, Gabon, Ghana, Togo, Guinea, Guinea-Bissau, Mali, Nigeria and Senegal – providing financial services in insurance and banking. With 12 non-life subsidiaries and eight life subsidiaries, and revenues of XOF152b, the insurance arm of NSIA controlled over 70% of the group's business, with the banking subsidiaries NSIA Banque Cote d'Ivoire and NSIA Banque Guinea (Conakry) contributing the balance to the group's business.

NSIA Banque Côte d'Ivoire, one of the top three largest banks in Côte d'Ivoire, came into existence in 2006 with NSIA's

---

78 http://www.forumafricanada.com/en/biographies-speakers/146-jean-kacou-diagou.html.

acquisition of BIAO-CI, while NSIA Banque Guinea was established in 2010.

In May 2016, NSIA increased its focus on corporate social responsibility with the signing of a convention between NSIA Foundation and the United Nations Fund for Population Activities (UNFPA), Côte d'Ivoire.

NSIA Participations

To effectively coordinate the strategy, policy direction, execution, human and financial resources, capital raising, shared services, business and operational activities of the group, NSIA Participations was created as a holding company and staffed with appropriate resources to manage these responsibilities. To further deepen its privatisation programme and reduce its stake in 15 state-owned enterprises, the government of Côte d'Ivoire decided, in 2013, to sell its 10% stake in BIAO-CI/ NSIA Banque, with 5% of the shares to be sold through the regional stock exchange (BVRM), while the balance 5% will be held by the cocoa and coffee marketing board, the Coffee and Cocoa Council.[79]

In its regional expansion drive into other parts of Africa, NSIA acquired 80% of the shares of CDH Insurance, a leading non-life insurance company in Ghana in 2010, with the expectation that NSIA's takeover will make the company a major player in the insurance sector in Ghana.[80]

---

79 Ivory Coast government approves sale of stake in NSIA Banque-http://www.reuters.com/article/ivorycoast-bank-(Reporting by Loucoumane Coulibaly; Writing by Joe Bavier; Editing by Marine Pennetier and David Holmes).
80 NSIA takes over CDH Insurance https://www.modernghana.com/news/265106/nsia-takes-over-cdh-insurance.html

In a move to strengthen its international capacity, NSIA Participations announced on 25 March 2015 the sale of 20.9% of its shareholding to National Bank of Canada, and 5.4% to Amethis Finance, which was previously held by the private equity firm, Emerging Capital Partners, with its ECP Fund III. NSIA brought to the table its "25 subsidiaries, 58 bank branches, 42 insurance agencies and assets totalling more than 1.2 billion euros".[81] According to NSIA's President, Jean Kacou Diagou, "We are very pleased to partner with National Bank of Canada, and we are very supportive of its development project for Africa, its financial strength and ethical and governance requirements. This partnership is a long-term alliance intended to create value for both of our institutions and promote economic development in Africa. The participation of Amethis Finance, an investment vehicle specialised in Africa, is an additional asset for NSIA."[82]

Affirming the long-term plans of Groupe NSIA, the Chairman, in an interview in Dakar, stated that NSIA had an ambition to become an international financial group, expanding beyond West and Central Africa, with plans to commence operations in DRC, Angola, Mozambique as well as East Africa.[83]

---

81 National Bank of Canada Purchases an Equity Stake in the African Financial Group NSIA Montreal - PRESS RELEASE. 25 March 2015. See also …. www…. Amethyst……

82 ibid.

83 For the full interview, see Le groupe NSIA n'est pas à vendre http://www.reussirbusiness.com/2015/04/24/jean-kacou-diagou-nsia-le-groupe-nsia-nest-pas-a-vendre/.

PART VI

INDUSTRIALISING AFRICA

Chapter Ten

CEMENTING AFRICA –
THE DANGOTE GROUP

In the 21st Century, the Dangote Group has established itself, as a pan-African institution actively cementing Africa, with cement manufacturing companies in West, Central, East and Southern Africa.

Dangote Group's mission, to "touch the lives of people by providing their basic needs" simplifies a huge self-appointed mandate to reach people at their basic levels of need. The mission is neither restrictive in geography nor product category.

The driving force behind the Group is Aliko Dangote, who founded the company in 1978[84] by trading in commodities. The business model remained essentially the same until the period from 1997 upwards, when Dangote veered into manufacturing. The period between 2000 and 2003 was one of

---

84 Aliko Dangote - The Role of Business in Driving Sustainable Business Development – The Story of the Dangote Group. A Presentation to the Lagos Business School Executive Students, Lagos Nigeria, October 17, 2016.

growth sustenance, with a strategy of asset acquisition, capacity expansion, structure and business process improvement.

Between 2003 and 2007, Dangote Group became a large conglomerate, with revenues of over $1.6 billion, and had created separate subsidiary entities engaged in the production of sugar, salt, flour and pasta. The scale of the Group's operations is also immediately evident in the Nigerian Stock Exchange where, as at March 2016, the market capitalisation of Dangote companies crested N3,832 trillion out of the total market capitalisation of N8.91 trillion, a whopping 43% of the market.[85] Though this has reduced, as at June 2018, four companies in the Dangote Group – Dangote Cement, Dangote Sugar Refinery, Dangote Flour and Nascon Allied Industries – had a market capitalisation of N4.321 trillion out of the total market capitalisation of N14,008 trillion, representing over 30% of the total capitalisation of the Nigerian Stock Exchange.[86]

Since 2007, the Group has focused on diversifying the business model from a Nigerian-focused cement business to a pan-African conglomerate, with an expanded product line that has interests in oil and gas, petrochemicals, agriculture and fertiliser in several African countries. By 2015 the Dangote Group's annual revenues had reached $3.2 billion.

At a presentation to executive students of Lagos Business School, Aliko Dangote outlined five factors guiding the group's business philosophy:

---

85 Dangote Group Controls 43% of Nigerian Stock Market by Goddy Egene in *Thisday* Newspapers March 9, 2016. www.thisdaylive.com.

86 Dangote Group: Epitome Of Good Corporate Governance by Olushola Bello in *Leadership* Newspaper. June 12, 2018. https://leadership.ng/2018/06/12/dangote-group-epitome-of-good-corporate-governance/.

- Identifying where to play and providing basic needs
- Efficient execution
- Effective operations
- Strategic partnerships
- Development of human capacity.

Financial Capacity

Two measures of the Group's growing financial capacity are its ability to efficiently manage its indebtedness and to take on several large-scale and transformational projects concurrently.

In 2009, Dangote Cement paid up a debt of $1.1 billion. In 2010, the group paid an outstanding debt of $1.5 billion, displaying a capacity to meet its obligations and strengthening its capacity to do more. Thereafter, Dangote reached an agreement with a consortium of banks to raise about $9 billion to build a petroleum complex and fertiliser plant, and a petroleum refinery.

Dangote Cement now describes itself as "Africa's leading cement producer with nearly 46mta capacity across Africa", with three production facilities in Nigeria – at Obajana, Ibese and Gboko – accounting for 29.25mta. With investments of about $3 billion, the company also has production facilities and operational activities in Cameroon, Congo, Ghana, Ethiopia, Senegal, Sierra Leone, South Africa, Tanzania and Zambia, which contribute about 40% of production volumes and 31% of total company revenues respectively. This clearly validates the Dangote Group's pan-African strategy.[87] Dangote's goal is to attain production of 77mta, which will place the company as the sixth largest cement producer in the world from the 11th position, and a production capacity of 44mta.[88]

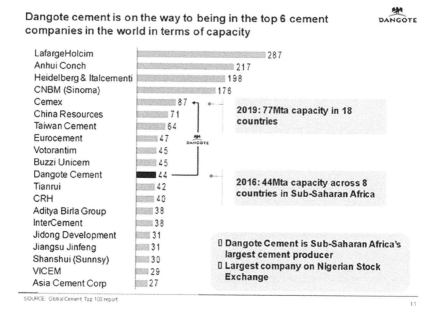

Dangote cement is on the way to being in the top 6 cement companies in the world in terms of capacity

LafargeHolcim	287
Anhui Conch	217
Heidelberg & Italcementi	198
CNBM (Sinoma)	176
Cemex	87
China Resources	71
Taiwan Cement	64
Eurocement	47
Votorantim	45
Buzzi Unicem	45
Dangote Cement	44
Tianrui	42
CRH	40
Aditya Birla Group	38
InterCement	38
Jidong Development	31
Jiangsu Jinfeng	31
Shanshui (Sunnsy)	30
VICEM	29
Asia Cement Corp	27

2019: 77Mta capacity in 18 countries

2016: 44Mta capacity across 8 countries in Sub-Saharan Africa

☐ Dangote Cement is Sub-Saharan Africa's largest cement producer
☐ Largest company on Nigerian Stock Exchange

SOURCE: Global Cement Top 100 report

11

Diverse Business Structure

A synergistic part of the Dangote conglomerate is its diverse and reinforcing nature. The group has business in cement, petrochemicals, gas, agriculture, sugar, power, telecommunications, salt, steel, food and beverages, pasta,

---

87 Dangote Cement Plc Announces Audited Results For The Year Ended 31st December 2017 in http://www.dangotecement.com/dangote-cement-plc-announces-audited-results-year-ended-31st-december-2017/; Unaudited results for the nine months ended 30th September 2018 in http://www.dangotecement.com/wp-content/ uploads/reports/2018/Q3/DangoteCement_Q32018_ResultsSta tement.pdf

88 Page 4 of http://www.dangotecement.com/wp-content/uploads/reports/2016/Q1/ DangoteCementGroup_Presentation-May2016.pdf

noodles, logistics, real estate, and others. At times, it is difficult to completely bifurcate or segregate the businesses. For instance, the company has more than 6,500 trucks in Nigeria and several thousands in other African countries. It is difficult to simply ascribe the trucks to the Group's cement, transport or logistics businesses, given their interrelatedness. Since 2007, the Dangote Group has begun a very active process of product and geographical expansion.

Product Diversity

Due to the sheer dominance of cement in the conglomerate's product bouquet, it is at times forgotten that there are other thriving and large business lines that the company engaged in long before it went into cement manufacturing. But Dangote, seeing advantages in backward integration and forward linkages, has veered into and consolidated its products lines.

Sugar

Dangote Sugar owns 150, 000 hectares (ha) of sugar plantations in Kwara, Kogi, Taraba Sokoto, Kebbi and Jigawa states, in Nigeria. In 2001, the company set up a sugar refining factory in Lagos, Nigeria, with a total capacity of 600,000 mt. With two expansion projects, the factory has increased capacity to 1.44 million mt per annum, which makes it the second largest sugar refinery in the world. In 2002, Dangote also acquired Savannah Sugar Company Limited, located in Numan, Adamawa State, which had a refining capacity of 50,000mta. Dangote Sugar plans to establish four new sugar refining factories in Nigeria, to make Nigeria self-sufficient in sugar production, with an investment plan of $1 billion, over ten years.

Petrochemicals

The Dangote petrochemical project is a statement in courage and audacity. The sheer size, complexity, integration and cost of the project amazes. The petrochemical complex is located in the Lekki Free Trade Zone in Lagos, Nigeria and is being constructed on a 2,100ha site. In monetary terms, the size of the project is estimated at $9 billion, which was the cost of the facility Dangote signed with a consortium of Nigerian and foreign banks. Aliko Dangote, in 2016, put the revised conservative cost at $12 billion, with a completion plan for 2018. However, this completion timeline was not met, and was moved forward. For crude oil, the plant has a capacity to refine 650,000 barrels per day, and will produce petroleum products like gasoline, jet fuel/kerosene, diesel, LPG, etc. The Dangote Group has stated that the complex is the largest "single standalone refinery in the world".

For fertiliser, the complex also has a 1.2mta polypropylene plant, as well as a 2.8mta urea and ammonia plant. The Dangote Group considers Nigeria's imports of about 500,000 mt and the local production of 1.6mta as inadequate to meet the country's agricultural requirements, which it estimates at about 5mta within the next five years. Working with partners such as SAIPEM and TATA, the fertiliser project which is being built on 500 ha at a cost of $2 billion, to produce 3 million tonnes p.a., has been described by Dangote as "the largest Granulated Urea Fertiliser complex coming up in the entire fertiliser industry history in the world." It also has a captive power plant, generating 120 MW and dedicated to meeting the power needs of the plants.

In summary, the Dangote Group worked simultaneously on six large-scale project initiatives in refinery and petroleum, fertiliser, a sub-sea gas pipeline, rice production, sugar production and capacity expansion in cement production – with a total investment outlay of $20 billion projected to create employment for 300,000 people.

The Dangote Group is driving 6 major projects which will create ~250 thousand jobs and provide FX earnings / savings of ~$15bn   DANGOTE

	Job creation[1] Est # of jobs	FX earnings / savings for the country Est USD bn		
				Savings Earnings
1 Refinery & petrochem	50k	6.0	6.0	12.0
2 Fertiliser	10k		0.5	0.4 0.9
3 Sub-sea gas pipeline	5k			0.0
4 Local rice production	30k[2]	Total investment of ~$20bn across the 6 projects	0.5	
5 Local sugar production	150k[2]		1.1	
6 Cement capacity expansion	5k			0.5
Total	250k	8.1	6.9	15.0

1 Direct and indirect jobs during construction & operations
2 Includes out-growers

12

Chapter Eleven

OILING AFRICA – OILIBYA

OiLibya[89] represents a generation of African institutions with operations and intentions in several parts of the continent. The company is owned by the Libyan State through the country's sovereign wealth fund, the Libyan Investment Authority.

The route to OiLibya's African expansion is traceable to the Libyan Investment Authority's acquisition, in 1988, of Tamoil, the trading brand of Oilinvest, a Dutch oil firm founded by the Lebanese-American, Roger Tamraz. Tamoil had refineries and over 3,000 service stations in different parts of Europe. It was Tamoil that launched its petroleum products retail business in Egypt.[90]

---

89 For a report on the history, profile, status, business and strategy of Oilibya, see www.oilibya.com.

90 COLLOMBEY REFINERY CLOSURE - Dramatic twist means Tamoil buyback may be possible.*Marc-André Miserez, Collombey* JUL 3, 2015 http://www.swissinfo. ch/eng/business/collombey-refinery-closure_dramatic-twist-means-tamoil-buyback-may-be-possible/41529676.

OiLibya has operations in 18 African countries and is engaged in downstream oil and gas operations, with over 1,000 fuel service stations providing retail petroleum products for commercial, marine and aviation users, with presence and services in 50 African airports. OiLibya also has eight lubricant blending plants in Morocco, Egypt, Tunisia, Cameroon, Senegal, Gabon, Kenya and Sudan, besides providing storage services and logistics.

A firm plan towards being a pan-African operating business kicked off between 2000 and 2004, with the set-up of Tamoil in Tchad, Niger, Mali and Burkina Faso, and the acquisition of Shell in Eritrea. Thereafter, the company went into a frenzy of acquisitions and purchased the Shell business in Niger, Tchad, Djibouti, Ethiopia and Sudan. The agreement to acquire 100% of the Ethiopian and Djibouti businesses was made in July 2008, following Shell's decision to exit the petroleum products retail business and focus on upstream oil and gas business. Shell had been in operation since 1929 in Ethiopia, with 200 service stations and a market share of about 30%.[91]

Furthermore, the company acquired ExxonMobil operations in Niger, Senegal, Côte d'Ivoire, Gabon, Cameroon, Kenya, Réunion, Tunisia and Morocco. It still partners with ExxonMobil, as it remains the distributor of Mobil lubricants in Morocco, Tunisia, Kenya, Cameroon, Côte d'Ivoire, Gabon, Senegal, Ethiopia and Libya.

Through its Dubai-based supply and trading subsidiary, Libya Oil Supply DMCC (LOS), it runs a global energy business in

---

91 OIL REPORT | Tue Jul 15, 2008 6:10pm BST - OiLibya buys Shell's Ethiopia, Djibouti operations. http://uk.reuters.com/article/ethiopia-libya-shell- idUKL159 192220080715

Africa, the Mediterranean and Asia. In July 2016, its Tunisian subsidiary acquired 34% shareholding of Lubrifiants de Tunisie (LDT).

OiLibya has become a pan-African corporation. In the same vein, the company has also changed its name, rebranded and become OLA (Oil Libya Africa) Energy. It pledged that it "will continue to deliver on its reputation as a dynamic pan-African retailer with an unrivalled portfolio of products and services in its operating markets", and committed to retain its "spirit of African business delivering the highest international quality standards" and "a brand created and driven by Africans, for Africans."[92]

---

92 OLA Energy – Network of Retail Outlets and Petroleum Products www.olaenergy. com

Chapter Twelve

THE AROMA OF AFRICA: BABA DANPULLO – TEA OF CAMEROON

The undulating hills of Ndawara in North West Cameroon welcome you to thousands of hectares of the lush and well-manicured green yards of tea plantations nurtured by Baba Danpullo.

Until he was named the richest man in Francophone Africa, with an estimated net worth of close to $1 billion, Baba Danpullo, a self-effacing business-man, was almost incognito in Africa – although he was well known in his home country, Cameroon. Variously described as humble and soft-spoken, Danpullo's business interests are along three main lines:

- Agriculture: tea production, livestock breeding, etc.
- Telecommunication
- Real estate development.

The Aroma of Tea

Tea is the group's best known and best-kept secret. With three plantations in Tole, Ndu and Djutittsa, lying respectively at 2000m, 1800m, 1500m above sea level, the Cameroon Tea Estates (CTE), operating from high altitude, produces a variety of tea products from volcanic-laden soil for local consumption and exports.[93]

The Tole tea, from the Tole Plantation, has been in operation since 1928 and is the oldest of the tea plantations in the Baba Danpullo Group. The Ndu plantation, on the other hand, which was set up in 1967, produces over 1800 mt of tea annually. It is located about 600 kilometres from Tole. The Ndu plantation, which lies on the highlands of Northwest Cameroon, was set up in 1956 by a British company, Estate and Agency, but it faced worker strikes and was managed by the government. Eventually, it was taken over by the Cameroon Development Corporation in 1977.

The Djutittsa plantation, which produces 2500 mt over a land mass of 445 hectares, is the youngest plantation, having come into existence in 1971.[94]

The story of tea in Cameroon is an interesting one. The Germans introduced tea in Limbe, then Victoria, in Southwest Cameroon. However, the implantation of tea took place at two different stages. First, a test plot was planted in Tole at the foot

---

93 For the evolution of the Tea in Cameroon, See http://www.ctetea.com/about-us. htm; Cameroonian Tea Experience, Mulutaki Achiri Robert Production Director Cameroon Tea Estates

94 Ibid

of Mount Cameroon, near Buea, in 1928. The tea was a hybrid of the Assam light-leaf tea and the dark-leaf Manipuri tea.

The second phase started in 1954 with the proper development and commoditisation of tea, with the launch of Tole Tea Estate and the cultivation of hectares of tea plantation.[95]

Tole, Ndu and Djutittsa tea estates, managed by Cameroon Development Corporation, were privatised in 2002. The Ndawara Highland Tea Estate, located 2,000 mt above sea level, sits on 1,643 hectares.[96]

Telecommunications

In Telecoms, Danpullo Group, utilising the investment vehicle Bestinver Asset Management acquired 30% shareholding in Viettel Cameroon,[97] which was later increased to 49%.[98] Viettel, operating under the brand Nexttel,[99] is the third largest mobile operating company in Cameroon, owned principally by the Vietnamese national telecommunication company. The company, which was licensed in 2012, commenced operations in September 2014, and by 2016 – two years later – it had three million subscribers, with over 75% coverage of the national territory. Its rapid expansion trajectory has continued, and in

---

95 Ibid

96 Ibid

97 http://www.nexttel.cm

98 Baba Ahmadou Danpullo: Africa's discreet business magnate by Paul Trustfull in https://www.worldfinance.com/markets/baba-ahmadou-danpullo-africas-discreet-business-magnate

99 Viettel Cameroon to operate under Nexttel brand https://www.telegeography.com/products/commsupdate/articles/2014/08/12/viettel-cameroon-to-operate-under-nexttel-brand/

November 2017, it crossed the four million subscriber mark – after three years of operations. [100] It had also invested over XAF250 billion or over $400 million in its network expansion programme, and created 1,000 jobs, and over 60,000 secondary jobs.[101] Other telecommunication companies which also competed for but did not win the third private sector operating licence for Cameroon included Maroc Telecom and Bharti Airtel, with operations in many African countries.

Real Estate

The group owns and runs residential and commercial real estate holdings in several countries, especially Cameroon, Nigeria, South Africa and Switzerland.

In South Africa, Baba Danpullo Group is reputed to own "the largest portfolio of independent properties in South Africa".[102] The group owns two malls in Cape Town and Johannesburg, the Mitsubishi Head Office Complex in Nelson Mandela Square (bought from Stocks and Stocks in 2000) and Marble Towers in Johannesburg, a 32-story building acclaimed to be the third tallest building in South Africa and the 6th tallest building in Africa.[103]

---

100 Cameroon: Nexttel exceeds 4 million subscribers in 3 years in Business in Cameroon. https://www.businessincameroon.com/telecom/1811-7570-cameroon-nexttel-exceeds-4-million-subscribers-in-3-years.

101 Baba Ahmadou Danpullo: Africa's discreet business magnate by Paul Trustfull in https://www.worldfinance.com/markets/baba-ahmadou-danpullo-africas-discreet-business-magnate.

102 Ibid.

103 Omer Mbadi Ahmadou in *Danpullo, the discreet emperor of Cameroonian business http: //www. jeuneafrique.com /17881/ economie/baba-ahmadou-danpullo-l-empereur-discret-du-business-camerounais August 7, 2013 and Business in Cameroon, November 4, 2015.*

Danpullo also has three shopping malls in South Africa. He acquired Moffet on Main Retail Centre in 2010, increasing his estate holdings in Port Elizabeth. This is after the acquisition of King's Court, a retail Centre.[104] A shrewd businessman, he had paid R57 million for the Mandela Bay Shopping Complex that was constructed for R300 million. This amount was less than 20% of the initial cost of the complex, purchased within the previous two years.

---

104 http://www.postnewsline.com/2010/05/south-africa-cameroonian-snaps-up-kings-court-bargain.html Friday, 07 May 2010 South Africa: Cameroonian snaps up King's Court bargain.

Chapter Thirteen

AFRICA'S METAL FOUNDATIONS: ALUMINUM AND STEEL – THE COMCRAFT GROUP

My first encounter with the Comcraft Group was in the mid-1990s when, as a relationship officer in Ecobank, I prospected and managed the business relationships of Tower Aluminum, Midland Galvanizing and Kolorkote Industries Ltd. – member companies of the Comcraft Group in Nigeria. In addition to the sizeable business generated by the companies, I found the general layout, design and ambience of their premises very welcoming.

The group remained true to its calling, with a strong focus on and specialisation in aluminum and steel, even after 70 to 80 years of operations in the sector.[105]

---

105 This chapter relied on information and excerpts from several reports on the history, profile, status, business and strategy of Manu Chandaria and the Comcraft Group see Knowledge@Wharton June 30, 2013.
Howwemadeitinafrica.com Dinfin Mulupi, October 15, 2013.

History and Migration

The history of the formation of the Comcraft Group[106] began in 1915 with the emigration and relocation of the patriarch of the Chandaria family, Manu Chandaria's father, from Gujarat, India to set up a provisions store on Biashara Street, in Nairobi, Kenya. Over time, and with greater financial stability, the larger family, consisting of a team of ten, including Manu's future father-in-law, acquired Kenya Aluminum, or Kaluworks, a company that manufactured aluminum cooking and roofing products.[107]

After his foundational education in Nairobi and Mombasa, Kenya, bachelor's degree at Jamnagar University in India in 1949 and postgraduate engineering education at the University of Oklahoma in the US in 1951, Manu joined the family aluminum business.[108]

In an interview with Creating Emerging Markets in *Harvard Business Review*, Manu Chandaria acknowledged that his parents waded through poverty in their entrepreneurial journey and had only the very basic lifestyle, stating wryly that when he "was born, there were spoons in the house but not silver or gold",[109] but that Kenya presented a new platform to "build and flourish".

---

106 Ibid.
107 Knowledge@Wharton: June 30, 2013.
108 *Creating Emerging Markets*, in Harvard Business Review, June 13, 2014. Interview with Henry McGee.
109 Ibid.

Expansion, Growth and Diversification

Starting in the 1950s, and continuing in the 1960s, the Comcraft Group began a process of extending its product base and expanding its operating countries. The company's products were exported to Tanzania, Uganda, Zambia, and the then Belgian Congo, now DRC. To protect its markets, as independence approached in many countries – and given the possibility that the newly independent countries would demand for investment rather than just being mere product receptacles, which could precipitate the loss of the company's long-established markets – the company set up operations in those countries. In five years, the company was already a pan-East African company. Comcraft also expanded to Nigeria, Ethiopia, Congo, Zambia, India, Singapore, the US, UK, etc. The group is currently in over 40 countries.[110]

In the initial expansion phase, the company focused on its core product, metal, and deployed family members to the new countries of operation. In its expansion to the UK and Europe, Comcraft deployed mainly an acquisition strategy to grow the business, essentially because industries and markets were very different from the ones in Africa. The group explored expansion opportunities, and in 2012, one of its subsidiaries, Kaluworks issued a corporate bond of $14 million.[111] In 2014, Comcraft announced its intention to expand its Kenyan business by 50% within three years, while building more factories. In Ethiopia, the group plans to increase the number of its factories from three to nine. Even in Nigeria, where it has been present since

---

110 Ibid; Creating Emerging Markets.
111 www.forbes.com. April 9, 2014. Kenya Mulitimillionaire Says He Plans to List Some Companies by Mfonobong Nsehe

the 1950s and has more than 4,000 employees, Comcraft still seeks to grow, to continually tap into the country's burgeoning population. It is important to highlight that the Group has faced severe financial and operational difficulties in Nigeria.[112]

Business Challenges – Capital

To overcome its capital constraints in its new market expansion strategy to purchase equipment and raw materials for production and sale, the company acquired equipment on a long-term credit basis, while raw materials were bought on a six-month credit basis. Critically, the company built and strengthened its reputation by meeting obligations on time – specifically, two days ahead of due date. There was also an uncompromising focus on quality and strong supplier relationship management and customer satisfaction.

These strategies enabled the company to stretch the capacity of its capital and replicate its strength in many markets.

Business Challenges – Global Economic Crises

The 2008 global economic crisis affected Comcraft's operations in Europe and North America, as the markets became vulnerable and Comcraft's business shrunk. Nonetheless, the benefits of diversification became evident as the company was able to meet the demand for its products due to the spread of its operations.

---

112 http://www.reuters.com/article/us-africa-summit-comcraft-
AFRICA INVESTMENT 2014 | Wed Apr 9, 2014 | 4:02am EDT Kenya's Comcraft
   Group discussing possible share offerings-chairman

Business Challenges: Government Policy Changes – Nationalisation

In recounting the difficulties encountered by the company in its early days, with the nationalisation of its assets in Ethiopia and Uganda, following governmental changes, and even in Congo and Burundi where Comcraft had to "abandon our assets", the assertion by Manu Chandaria was profound: *In business you cannot keep animosity in your mind because of actions beyond your control.* That way, the company was able to pare down its losses and retain focus on the larger long-term opportunities in Ethiopia where it continued business, in Rwanda where it set up a manufacturing outfit, and in Burundi where it set up a marketing office.[113]

In Nigeria, the flagship business – though severely challenged with financial and operational constraints – was Tower Aluminum Group, which became operational in 1959 and manufactures building products like roofing sheets, extruded profiles, billets, rolled and colour-coated coils and kitchenware. With presence also in Mali, Guinea Conakry, Burkina Faso, Ghana, Côte d'Ivoire and Benin, at its peak, Tower Aluminum prided itself as "the single largest vertically integrated aluminum downstream producer and a pioneer in West Africa".[114]

Giving

The Chandaria Foundation, which was set up way back in the 1950s, is the charity and corporate social responsibility arm of the Comcraft Group, chaired directly by Manu Chandaria, and

---

113 Op cit. Creating Emerging Markets
114 www.towerplc.com

with charitable trusts in each operating country. The Foundation has sponsored several schools and hospitals in the group's home country – Kenya. At the United States International University (USIU), there is the Chandaria School of Business, while at the Kenyatta University, there is the Chandaria Business Innovation and Incubation Centre. It is estimated that he has donated over $100 million to charitable causes in his lifetime.[115] Manu Chandaria posits that growth and profitability places a responsibility on businesses to invest in society, especially in education and health. This is also an important ingredient of business success.[116]

---

115 FORBES APR 9, 2014
116 Knowledge@Wharton

Chapter Fourteen

MODERNISING AFRICAN ENTREPRENEURSHIP: THE TONY ELUMELU FOUNDATION

The Tony Elumelu Foundation (TEF)[117] was set up in 2010 by Tony O. Elumelu (CON) when he, along with other bank CEOs, was compelled to face early retirement – following a regulatory decision capping the tenure of bank CEOs. Prior to that, he was the GMD/CEO of United Bank for Africa, a pan-African bank which had emerged from its merger with Standard Trust Bank, a rapidly rising new generation bank, and the acquisition of some challenged Nigerian banks through a process of Purchase and Assumption, midwifed by the Central Bank of Nigeria. UBA was undergoing a rapid-fire expansion programme across Africa.

Because of its proximate relationship with the bank, and given that the founder was the chairman of the bank, some of the

---

117 For information on the programmes and initiatives of Tony Elumelu Foundation, see www.tonyelumelufoundation.org

Foundation's outreach programmes are sometimes associated with the bank.

Following its launch, the Foundation initiated many programmes and signed many partnership agreements. However, the TEF's flagship outreach initiative is the TEF Entrepreneurship Programme. Primarily, it has a vision to "establish the pre-eminent pan-African entrepreneurship programme and create 10,000 startups across Africa within 10 years that will generate significant employment and wealth". To achieve this ambition, TEF proposed to create businesses that would generate $10 billion in revenue and employ 1,000,000 new workers over a ten-year period. Under the programme, the Foundation provides a grant of $10,000 to identified entrepreneurs with viable business ideas, using a screening process managed by Accenture. The only criterion for selection is the viability of the proposed ideas. The programme, which is well advertised in print, electronic and digital media, has also become very popular.

A measure of the enormous interest generated, and the awareness created by the TEF was that in commemoration of the 5th anniversary and the 5th cohort of the programme in 2019, the Foundation announced the selection of a record 3,050 applicants from a record applicants of over 261,000.[118] The Foundation, through partnerships with institutions like the Red Cross, AfDB, UNDP, the governments of Benin Republic,

---

118 TONY ELUMELU FOUNDATION ANNOUNCES 3,050 ENTREPRENEURS SELECTED FOR THE 5th CYCLE OF THE TEF ENTREPRENEURSHIP PROGRAMME; https://tonyelumelufoundation. org/press-releases/tony-elumelu-foundation-announces-3050-entrepreneurs-selected-for-the-5th-cycle-of-the-tef-entrepreneurship-programme

and Botswana, Anambra State government, and Indorama, increased the number of awardees from the designated slots of 1000 to 3050. Importantly also, the 2019 cohort had more gender balance with almost 90,000 female applicants and female award representation of 41.6.%, and a spread in economic sectors with agriculture providing 29%, ICT – 8.7%, education and training – 7.6%, manufacturing – 7.5%, commercial/retail – 7.5%, fashion – 6.8% and healthcare – 5.1%.

It was the 4th cycle, in 2018, which had 151,692 applications that for the first time since commencement, selected an additional 250 eligible entrepreneurs funded and supported by new partners. In a fillip to employment generation, the Tony Elumelu Foundation states that its premier entrepreneurship programme has created over 55,000 jobs in Africa since the commencement of the scheme in 2015. A testament to its increasing acceptance and popularity is the rapid growth in the base of applicants. In 2015, the first year, there were over 20,000 applicants from 52 countries. In 2016 the applicants had grown to over 45,000 from 54 countries, with another batch of 1,000 being selected. In the third year, 2017, the number had grown exponentially to 93,000 entrepreneurs, with another batch of 1,000 being selected. Significantly, the successful applicants represent a bold and diverse community of Africans.

Each of the winners is exposed to a 12-week intensive training programme consisting of direct, video and online sessions on management, product design, sales, marketing, etc., and a bootcamp, all aimed at providing the entrepreneurs with the requisite skills, tools and experienced mentors required to facilitate the effective management of their businesses. The programme culminates in the TEF Entrepreneuership

Forum, which takes place yearly, with the participation of the 1,000 winners. There are presentations, bonding, networking and mentoring sessions by entrepreneurs, corporate leaders, scholars, senior government officials and even presidents of African countries. Selected entrepreneurs are provided with non-returnable seed capital funding of an initial $5,000. Successful resource management and business growth guarantees eligibility for an additional seed returnable amount of $5,000.

During trips to African countries, Tony Elumelu meets with past and present winners of the scheme in these countries, and where practicable, introduces them directly to the presidents of their countries. In October 2016, I participated as a guest speaker in the TEF Forum that took place at the auditorium of the Nigerian Law School, in Lagos. I told the participants that, with commitment and focus, there are really no impediments to achieving their personal and corporate goals. I also discussed access to finance by existing businesses, and funding for start-ups, and how existing businesses can raise working and long-term financing to grow sustainable businesses that will impact communities, countries and, ultimately, the African continent.

In July 2018, the Tony Elumelu Foundation hosted an interactive session with President Macron of France, with over 2,000 entrepreneurs in attendance, in Lagos. Similarly, the fourth edition of the TEF Forum, which took place in October 2018, and attracted entrepreneurs, business and government leaders, also had an interactive session moderated by Tony Elumelu and anchored by Presidents Nana Akufo-Addo of Ghana and Uhuru Kenyatta of Kenya. President Uhuru Kenyatta also made a keynote presentation by video conference. Significantly, the forum witnessed the successful launch of TEFConnect, a digital entrepreneurship platform that, expectedly, will bring together African entrepreneurs in one ecosystem.

The 2019 Forum on 26 and 27 July 2019, in Abuja, Nigeria had Presidents Macky Sall of Senegal, Paul Kagame of Rwanda, and President Felix Tshisekedi of Congo DR participating in the Founder's Dialogue.

TEF has, through focused and impactful giving and a healthy dose of differentiation, branding, digital communication and profound storytelling, become a leading proponent of entrepreneurship and philanthropy in Africa.

PART V

MINDWARE IN AFRICA

Mindware is the software of pan-African integration in the 21st century and represents a major and current expression and facilitator of integration in Africa. It is soft because it is based on access to the mind. In essence, it is soft power. It is software because it increasingly relies on technology for its manifestation or distribution. Mindware relies on the use and deployment of digital capabilities to create, develop, enrich and disseminate content. This has also facilitated the growth, reach and impact of "NEST" – Nollywood, Entertainment, Sports, and the Temple in Africa.

Chapter Fifteen

AFRICAN FILM AND MOVIE INDUSTRY

Origins

The African film and movie industry has had multidimensional origins, sprouts and manifestations. In precolonial times, there were no films and movies anywhere. However, Africans expressed entertainment, arts and culture in paintings, carvings, music, dance, family and communal engagements, storytelling by elders, griots, etc. These events took place regularly, and though not electronically recorded, as there were no such devices at that time, historical records and documents were kept by elders and community historians.

The production of films, videos and electronic records is a recent phenomenon in world history. Voice recording came with the invention of the phonautograph[119] by Édouard-Léon Scott de Martinville. Thomas Edison came with the

---

119 History of recording http://www.http://charm.rhul.ac.uk/history/p20_4_1hmtle trust.org/about/history-of-recording/

phonograph in 1877,[120] followed by a series of other inventions and improvements by several scientists up till the 20th century when the technology was perfected.

Though we have ancient wall and rock inscriptions, tablet writings, manifest paintings, sculptures and monuments still existing, other great accomplishments in different parts of the pre-historical, historical and ancient world have limited documentation, as there were no electronic records then. The world is now able to support history indirectly through technology and carbon-dating of historical events, activities and relics.

Tales of great accomplishments by communities and kingdoms have been told and retold, such that they have become ingrained in the hearts and minds of existing generations and transmitted to future generations. For Africans, the minds of men and women were vast libraries. Rocks and the walls of cities became the canvas of history, for record-keeping.

During the colonial era, movie-making and the film industry were not really the focus of the colonial powers in Africa i.e., the British, French, Portuguese, Spanish and Italians. Nonetheless, in the early 20th century, the French, as part of a larger cultural outreach, encouraged and supported the growth of a film industry in Francophone Africa. This was manifested in literature, poetry, drama and other documented writings. This also led to the emergence of several prominent Francophone actors, actresses, film producers and directors like Ousmane Sembène, Souleymane Cissé, etc.

---

120 http://charm.rhul.ac.uk/history/p20

There is little evidence that the British, Portuguese, Spanish or Italians showed any sustained interest in the early development of movies and film-making in their colonial territories. However, the struggle for independence led to various manifestations of pan-African nationalism, including film and moviemaking.

Morocco

The Moroccan film industry is emerging as a leading centre for film production in Africa. Morocco has leveraged on its geographical location, picturesque landscape, unique topography and relative peace and stability to differentiate the country as a conducive environment and destination for international filmmaking in Africa. Several ancient, historical, biblical, pharaonic and Arabian movies have been, and continue to be filmed, in Morocco. Even movies based on events in far-flung places outside North Africa and the Middle East have been shot in Morocco.

Ouarzazate in south central Morocco, aptly described as the "door of the desert" because of its location as a gateway to the Sahara Desert, is the popular destination for film production in Morocco.

The Moroccan government has established the Moroccan Cinema Centre to provide structured support to the film industry. Among other things, the institute provides scenic locations for film-making. The government of Morocco also provides incentives and tax rebates for foreign filmmakers with the stated intent of facilitating film production in the country. The incentives are working, as there are more productions and an increased impact of the cinema in the cultural and social activities in the country.

Since independence, African countries have taken several and diverse paths. Nonetheless, South Africa, Egypt, Morocco and Nigeria have emerged as powerhouses in film and media production. Others are emerging – Burkina Faso, Senegal, Mali, Cameroon, Ghana, Côte d'Ivoire, Kenya, DR Congo, Congo Brazzaville, Tanzania, Uganda, Gabon and many others. The future and direction of the film industry in Africa is the emergence of film citywoods and countrywoods beyond Nollywood and Kannywood in Nigeria, Riverwood in Kenya, and Ghollywood in Ghana.

Film Festivals

A growing trend is the staging of film festivals in different parts of Africa. The film festivals provide showcase opportunities for talents, actors, actresses, producers, directors and cinematographers in the movie industry. New movie productions are presented to eager audiences. Excellent productions are highlighted, and where appropriate, awards are given. The film festivals include FESPACO, that takes place in Ouagadougou in Burkina Faso; Cape Town International Film Market and Festival (CTIFM&F) in Cape Town, South Africa; Durban International Film Festival (DIFF) in Durban, South Africa; Nairobi Film Festival in Nairobi, Kenya; Africa International Film Festival in Lagos, Nigeria; Zanzibar International Film Festival in Zanzibar, Tanzania; Rwanda Film Festival in Kigali; Cairo International Film Festival in Cairo, Egypt; Carthage Film Festival in Tunis, Tunisia; and several others. Interestingly, there are also several film festivals and award ceremonies that take place outside Africa, mainly in Europe and North America, and they showcase the African movie industry. They include Toronto International Film Festival in Toronto; New York African Film Festival in New York; New African Film Festival in Washington DC; Afrika Eye Film Festival and Film Africa, both in London; and many more. Interestingly, Film Africa proudly proclaims itself as the "UK's largest festival of African film and culture", engaged in "celebrating the best African cinema from the continent."[121]

The acclaimed Cannes Film Festival in France also features Nollywood films and a section of the event screens African movies.

FESPACO

Festival Panafricain du Cinéma et de la télévision de Ouagadougou (FESPACO)[122] is the largest film festival in Africa. Held biennially, FESPACO is also the oldest surviving film festival in Africa, having started in 1969. The highlight of each Festival is the award of the premier prize, *L'Etalon de Yennenga,* i.e., the Golden Stallion, which was instituted in 1972. That year also, a permanent secretariat for FESPACO was set up. In 1982, initiatives continued to institutionalise FESPACO, with the establishment of the First African International Film and TV Market, the resuscitation of the pan-African Filmmakers Federation (FEPACI) and the opening of the African Film Library of Ouagadougou in 1985. In 2005, the base of recognition expanded and many additional award categories were introduced.

---

121 www.filmafrica.uk.org
122 www.fespaco.bf

FESPACO also receives funding and support from the government of Burkina Faso, as it became a government institution in 1972. The President of Burkina Faso, Roch Marc Kabore, proclaimed that the festival is "the best vehicle for culture in our continent." Similarly, the mayor of Ouagadougou, FESPACO's host city, Armand Béouindé, described the city as "the city of creativity, the city of culture, and the capital of African film." Such energy and effusion is evident in the impact of the event in the country and the city. Though with routine and usual logistical challenges in the organisation of FESPACO, progress is being made. In 1969, at commencement, only 23 movies from five African countries were featured, while in 2017, about 1,000 movie submissions were received. Importantly, the African diaspora is now eligible to participate and compete in the festival's prizes. During FESPACO's 50th anniversary in 2019, there 10,000 participants and 450 screenings with *Mercy of the Jungle*, a Rwandan film by Joel Karekezi, winning the coveted the Golden Stallion award.[123]

FESPACO remains focused on meeting its goal of promoting African culture, as it now attracts interest, participation and keen competition from all over the world.

Nairobi Film Festival[124]

One measure of the spread and reach of the African film and movie industry is the launch of the Nairobi Film Festival in

---

123 http://www.bbc.com/news/world-africa-March 3, 2017. Fespaco 2017: Six things about Africa's biggest film festival By Lamine Konkobo; https://www.theeastafrican.co.ke/magazine/Rwandan-film-wins-Fespaco-top-award/434746-5038996-y5d1hg/index.html
124 Business Daily March 30, 2018. P.30. www.bdafrica.com.

2017 by Sheba Hirst. The Festival also premiered *Mbithi Masya*, which went on to win several awards. An evidence of progress was witnessed in the second edition of the Film Festival in March 2018 which premiered three Kenyan films: *Supa Modo, New Moon* and *Disconnect*. Critically, the theme of the Festival was Contemporary African Cinema, with screened movies, cast, directorships, and shoot locations being essentially African. During the festival, there were films like *Walley* from Burkina Faso, *Vaya* from South Africa, *Wulu* from Mali and Guinea Conakry, *Silas* from Liberia, *Lilana* from Swaziland, *I Am Not a Witch* from Zambia, and *Walu Wote* from Kenya. Significantly, *Supa Modo* was selected as Kenya's entry for the 2019 Academy Awards, under the foreign language category.[125]

On its part, the Kenya Film Corporation has initiated measures to develop interest in and boost local production of films with a target of 40% utilisation of local content in film-making. The corporation plans to organise workshops in the entire 47 counties in the country, to encourage youths to take interest in film-making.[126]

In May 2018, *Rafiki,* a film produced in Kenya by Wanuri Kahiu, and based on the short story, *Jambula Tree,* by Monica Arac de Nyeko, was featured at the 2018 International Film Festival at Cannes and became the first film from East Africa to be screened at Cannes, and the only female-directed movie from Africa, inspite of the controversy surrounding its ban by the

---

125 Supa Modo' selected to represent Kenya in the Oscars by Hillary Kimuyu in *Daily Nation* – Kenya, October 7, 2018 in https://www.nation.co.ke/lifestyle/buzz/Supa-Modo-Oscars/441236-4794678-njon15z/index.html

126 97. Kenya Film Commission (KFC) moves to boost local content production in MyGov. June 12, 2018. P.2

Kenya Film Classification Board. It joined several Nollywood movies like *Adindu, Iterum, No Good Turn, Coat of Harm,* and other African movies to be screened at Cannes. Lagos, Nigeria's economic nerve centre also showcased the history and success of Nollywood in its documentary, *Nollywood in Lagos,*[127] featured at Cannes.

Multichoice Talent Factory[128]

Having emerged as a veritable entertainment medium and viable economic sector, the interest in and commitment to the film industry in Africa continues to grow. In May 2018, Multichoice Africa, part of Naspers, the South African media group engaged in the provision of direct-to-home television subscription entertainment programming in 49 African countries, joined other brands – DSTV, GOTV and Supersport – to launch the Multichoice Talent Factory (MTF). The initiative is geared

---

127 For coverage on participation at Cannes, see also Behind the Scenes of 'Rafiki' at Cannes in *The East African,* May 26 – June 1, 2018. P vi – vii. http://www.pulse.ng/entertainment/movies/2016-cannes-film-festival-4-nigerian-films-screening-at-69th-edition-id5021752.html;(https://lifestyle.thecable.ng/coat-harm-cannes-film-festival/) http://punchng.com/experts-hail-nigerian-movie-industry-at-cannes/.

128 See the following, etc., on the Multichoice Talent Factory
http://multichoicetalentfactory.com/Home/
Times of Zambia June 1, 2018, pg 11.
https://www.lusakatimes.com/2018/05/30/multichoice-announces-a-major-pan-african-initiative-for-film-television-industry/
https://www.opportunitiesforafricans.com/multichoice-talent-factory-film-skills-development-programme-2018/
http://www.kbc.co.ke/multichoice-launches-talent-factory-academy-targeting-film-tv-creatives/.
https://economist.com.na/35592/extra/multichoice-talent-factory-for-the-creative-industry-launched/.
http://nigeriacommunicationsweek.com.ng/multichoice-plans-talent-factory-initiative/.

towards training and nurturing talent over a 12-month period. Starting with 60 students from 13 African countries – Angola, Botswana, Ethiopia, Ghana, Kenya, Malawi, Mozambique, Nigeria, Namibia, , Tanzania, Uganda, Zambia and Zimbabwe – this capacity-building initiative is intended to "ignite Africa's creative industries" by providing both academic and practical experience in cinematography, film editing, audio production and storytelling. The programme will be activated through the MTF Academy that will operate from Lagos, Nigeria; Nairobi, Kenya; and Lusaka, Zambia.

I expect that Multichoice will imbibe lessons from the inaugural phase of the talent factory and expand the base from the initial 13 participating countries to include other non-English speaking countries, and also make the MTF an annual programme. This will ensure greater diversity, inclusion, reach and impact.

Though conceived as a social investment programme and funded by Multichoice, the MTF will create opportunities for skills acquisition and talent development that can immediately be deployed to work in television and movie production. Relatedly, the skilled and experienced professionals who will emerge from the talent factory could set up their production and service firms, which would further deepen capacity and build the film and movie industry as a viable economic sector in Africa.

Chapter Sixteen

NOLLYWOOD

Nollywood has become the largest and most authentic socio-cultural export from Africa in the 21st century. It has redefined the perception of Nigerians and Africans, not only in Africa, but in all parts of the world. This has been accentuated by its growing acceptance by the African diaspora in Europe, North America and Asia, and by people of African descent in Western Europe and the Americas, especially in the Carribeans, Brazil, and others.

History

Nollywood, as a thematic industry, burst into the consciousness of Nigerians in 1992, following the production and release of the movie *Living in Bondage* by Kenneth Nnebue. The movie was not prepared for its eventual stardom and landmark role. Though it was shot over a period of two weeks, it sold over one million copies. The unplanned success of *Living in Bondage* led to enormous interest in the Nigerian movie industry.

It is important to emphasise that Nollywood and movie production did not start from a clean slate. The origins and interstices of Nollywood and the Nigerian movie industry can be found at three critical and interconnected levels:

- Production: theatre and drama
- Nigerian television
- Programming: Nigerian drama and soap opera

Production: Theatre and Drama

From the 1950s to the 1990s, theatre production and stage plays were very popular in Nigeria. It was developed into a profession and business by several pioneers including Hubert Ogunde, Jab Adu, Ola Balogun, Wole Amele, Duro Ladipo, Jimi Solanke, and others. Some like Hubert Ogunde had theatre production facilities in Lagos and different parts of the country. Some of them had moving theatre vans and embarked on tours to different parts of Lagos and Nigeria. They also staged major plays at the National Theatre, Iganmu, Lagos, which was the landmark event centre in Nigeria for the arts and other activities at that time.

Early and popular comperes like John Chukwu were also instrumental in the sprouting and gestation of the Nigerian arts scene and, subsequently, movie industry. Even radio and TV presenters and personalities like Ernest Okonkwo, Muyiwa Adetiba, Benson Idonije, Julie Coker, Sebastian Offurum, Moji Makanjuola, Danladi Bako, John Momoh, Sola Omole, Waheed Olagunju, Yinka Craig, Frank Olize, Cyril Stober, Ruth Benamasia, Kehinde Young Harry, Eugenia Abu, Augusta Ndiwe, Emeka Maduegbuna, and others nurtured in the broadcast media, were also critical pioneers. Ernest Okonkwo, as a football commentator, had the capacity, with his sonorous voice, analytical ability and descriptive prowess, to literally carry the listener into the field of play.

Nigerian Television

Another critical contributory factor to the emergence and rapid expansion of Nollywood into global presence, was the widespread and ubiquitous existence of Nigerian television. The first television station in Africa, WNTV, which also predated many television stations in different parts of the world, was set up in Ibadan in 1959. Thereafter, and following the decentralisation of the Nigerian system of government, the Nigerian Television Authority (NTA) was created in 1977. The NTA then took over the existing regional television stations in the country. Television stations were then established by the federal government of Nigeria in 12 states, later in 19 states, subsequently in 21 states, and then in 36 states of the Federation. Each state and the Federal Capital Territory had at least one NTA station. Lagos, given its cosmopolitan nature and large urban population, had at least four NTA stations, including NTA Channel 10, NTA 2 Channel 5, NTA Channel 7, and over ten privately owned television stations in the city.

NTA currently has over 100 television stations in Nigeria and prides itself as the largest television network in Africa.

Another development was the establishment of television stations by each state government in the country. The aim was to enable them air their perspectives directly to the citizens of their states. This became imperative when the central and state governments were controlled by different political parties and particular views had to be aired or contradicted.

The third level of the evolution of Nigerian television is the deregulation and liberalisation of broadcast media in Nigeria in 1992 as well as the emergence of specialisation across broadcast fields. This led to the issuance of broadcast licences to private sector players. The issuance of these licences led to the proliferation of television stations in Nigeria. Early-bird private sector players included, Degue Broadcasting Network (DBN), with a focus on sports; Channels, positioned as a news channel; Africa Independent Television (AIT), Silverbird Television (STV), Galaxy TV, MINAJ, MITV, Superscreen etc., focusing on entertainment, lifestyle and general interest. Some states had multiple television stations. Lagos, for instance, had about 15 television stations in 2017. These television stations, over time, began 24-hour broadcasts and created multiple options for viewers. Critically, the presence of numerous television stations in the country necessitated and compelled the existence of requisite skills, competence and capacity for film production and moviemaking.

Nigerian Drama and Soap Opera

In the 1980s and 1990s, television stations began to actively film and air Nigerian soap operas on local television stations and on the NTA network, usually on a weekly basis. These soap operas were humorous and fun-filled, parodying the lives of individuals and groups in Nigeria. They also promoted cultural values and reflected common themes that Nigerians were familiar with and experienced daily. Those on the NTA network were usually aired before the 9 p.m. network news broadcast. Viewers eagerly looked forward to watching these television series. The programmes included:

- *New Masquerade*
- *New Village Headmaster*
- *Behind the Clouds*
- *Cock Crow at Dawn*
- *Samanja*
- *Jaguar*
- *Sura the Tailor*
- *Hotel De Jordan*
- *Baba Sala*
- *The Sunny Side of Life*
- *Icheoku*

There were others like *Tales by Moonlight* which were neither drama nor soap operas, but folktales and lore from different parts of the country. *Newsline* was a Sunday evening diet in many Nigerian homes and consisted of a round-up of the softer side of life, activities and events in Nigeria by the legendary Frank Olize and later Yinka Craig and several other reputable anchors on news and entertainment.

Icheoku

Icheoku was a television series of a colonial court translator and court jester who, wearing a crisply-ironed shirt and shorts, frequently and very humorously (mis)interpreted the statements of the prosecution and defence, and the deliberations and judgements of the colonial court.

Village Headmaster

This story was set in a village and built around a school, its headmaster, students, teachers and a king who shuffled before he climbed to his throne of office. It had the village teacher Mr Garuba; the village gossip, Amebo, played by Ibidun Allison; and the loquacious Chief Eleyinmi played by Funsho Adeolu. A measure of the popularity of the drama and its larger socio-cultural impact is that *amebo* has become, and remains, a reference word for a gossip in Nigerian lingo.

New Masquerade

This was a long-running drama series on NTA. It was humor par excellence and centred around the family home of Chief Zebrudaya Okoroigwe Nwogbo alias 4.30, played by Chika Okpala, and his wife Madam Ovularia. But the real source of rib-cracks and unending laughter and the anchors of *New Masquerade* were the home workers – Clarus, played by Davis Offor and Gringori played by James Iroha. Their antics held viewers spellbound. Others in the mood-lifting cast were Jegede (Claude Eke), Natty and Apena.

Cock Crow at Dawn

This was set in the central Nigerian city of Jos and had a romantic theme. It was centred around the lives of Bitrus, played by the well-known Sadiq Daba, and Zemaye, played by Ene Oloja who, in spite of family restrictions and adversity, fought for love.

Hotel De Jordan

This drama series was set in Benin City, but was popular across midwestern Nigeria. Created by Joe Ihonde, it revolved around several characters – the rich and loud Chief Ajas (Sam Osemede), the humorous houseworkers – Idemudia (Agbonifo Enaruna) and Kokori (David Ariyo). Idemudia's acting skills competed with and complemented his singing prowess, as his songs were touching, searing to the soul and evoked compassion. Prof. Milo Moro, Bob Allan (Richard Idubor) and others were also part of the cast.

Different Times: Similar Themes

Like Nollywood, the themes of the TV drama series and soaps revolved around love and romance, crime and punishment, the role of family in society, work and reward, humor, results and recognition, the value of education, etc. Given the popularity of these drama series, and the large audience and followership they attracted, the cast and crew had respect, acclaim and fame.

Most of the leading programmes were broadcast on NTA and watched throughout the country. Living in Lagos in the mid-1980s, I watched these soaps regularly and was familiar with their themes and storylines.

How Did Nollywood Sprout in Nigeria?

Nollywood did not start from a *tabula rasa*, but was built on a strong platform with skilled professionals, a well-educated cast and crew, and highly entrepreneurial people. There were facilitative conditions. It was therefore inevitable, that Nigeria gave birth to a film industry in due course.

Population

With a population of 200 million people, Nigeria remains a veritable and ready consumer of well-produced products. Nollywood was a product ready to be consumed, given its familiar and affirmative themes and storylines as well as the ease of access of the movies and distribution.

Educational and Social System

The Nigerian educational system unwittingly prepares children and youths for professions in acting, drama, film production and related fields of endeavour. There are many stage plays in schools from popular Nigerian literature – *Things Fall Apart* by Chinua Achebe, Wole Soyinka's *Kongi's Harvest* and *The Lion and The Jewel*, Ola Rotimi's *The Gods Are Not To Blame*, *Isiburu* by Elechi Amadi, and numerous others. In my secondary school, Ika Grammar School Agbor, I was an actor in both *The Gods Are Not to Blame* and *Isiburu*. My school also visited other schools to stage plays. This method of teaching represents an active process of responsibility placement, socialisation and preparation in public and private schools in Nigeria. In spite of the passage of time, this practice continues. Though my experience was in a different era several decades ago, my kids have also undergone this process of preparation. Many schools in different parts of Nigeria are active in drama production, even going on to produce high-quality presentations and shows beyond the schools. Elurinmakiwehe, my daughter, performed in Ola Rotimi's classic, *The Gods Are Not To Blame*. Her school also led its students to stage the popular *Ovonramwen Nogbaisi* at the MUSON Centre in Lagos, where, as a ten-year-old, my daughter, Elumedon performed. Even at six years old, my son, Iyare III, played a part in the school's dramatisation of *Lion King*. This process of preparation continues in high schools.

Theatre production was also facilitated by the proliferation of theatre arts, dramatic arts, mass communication, creative arts, performing arts, visual arts and other related courses in Nigerian universities, polytechnics and other institutions of higher learning – thereby creating cognate interest and capacity to work in drama and film production. Most universities had theatre production crews and regularly staged plays for students and other interested members of the public. At the University of Lagos where I schooled, I witnessed many rehearsals, productions and performances at the university's arts theatre and main auditorium. This was undoubtedly the case in several other universities where plays were staged and regularly presented in arts' theatres.

The educational and social system encouraged arts and drama production in the educational curricula in primary schools, secondary schools and tertiary institutions. While they may not have been separate fields of study in school, at their levels, schools had drama clubs, literary and debating societies, etc. For many people, including me, the drama club was the first introduction to theatre production and drama, as we not only acted in stage plays in our high schools, but also went to nearby high schools to showcase our plays. A critical observation was that production was directed by fellow students who guided and led the entire process. Universities also had departments with various fields of engineering which provided facilitative skills and platforms for the take-off, growth and rapid expansion of theatre production, film production, and ultimately, Nollywood in Nigeria.

Literacy

The literacy rate of youth between 15 and 24 in Nigeria, which represents a very active segment of the population, was estimated by UNICEF[129] at 75.6% for males, 58% for females, and 51.1% for the total adult population – all between 2008 and 2012. In other words, while the non-literate population in Nigeria is high, the responsible government bodies in the country should adopt concerted and effective methods to completely eradicate illiteracy. Given that education is a direct source of self, community and national development and empowerment, the educated Nigerian population of about 100 million is significant.

For Nollywood, this was a population with the ready absorptive capacity to consume quality content.

The Church in Nigeria

The church, consisting of the Orthodox, Protestant, Pentecostal, and other denominations regularly staged plays and drama productions in which members of the congregation played roles as biblical characters. Furthermore, churches in Nigeria historically provided platforms for the development of periodically-produced drama sketches during special religious festivities to commemorate events like Christmas and Easter. During these periods, children and adults were assigned roles

---

129 www.unicef.org At a glance: Nigeria. Statistics

to represent biblical characters and personalities. These plays were then staged in churches during church programmes.

The Economy

The Nigerian economy witnessed tremendous growth at the turn of the millennium. With an economic size of $510 billion (2014), Nollywood and the arts represented 1.3% or about $6.63 billion of the GDP.[130]

The Diffusion of Nollywood

With the increase in purchasing power of the middle class, the reduction of the price of electronic gadgets and an increased access to television, smartphones, VCDs and DVDs, there is a generous and enhanced availability of content. Consequently, there are people who watch Nollywood movies on their computers, tablets and smartphones. My assessment is that there is a relationship between the total mobile phone penetration of over 160 million and a top-ten internet usage of about 100 million, and the digital dissemination and content uptake of Nollywood.

Nollywood - Role and Reach

Satellite Television

Given the increasing interest in Nollywood movies, film production and content development have become even more urgent. John Ugbe, the CEO of DSTV Nigeria says that "we

---

130 Mzwandile Jacks in Nollywood Contributes Massively To Nigeria's GDP www.venturesafrica.com. April 7, 2014.

have produced more local contents than we have ever done".[131] He also added that the Africa Magic channels which feature mainly Nollywood movies are "very popular, not just in Nigeria, but all over the continent",[132] and that from zero presence of Nollywood content on DSTV channels, Nollywood now has seven channels. The Nollywood channels have become so much in demand that the company had to move some popular football programming to lower bouquets.

Digital Nollywood

A growing percentage of viewers now access Nollywood through free-on-air and subscription-based digital platforms like iROKOtv, YouTube, Netflix, Amazon and numerous websites that offer free downloads of Nollywood movies. It is very common, even pedestrian, for me to visit a supermarket, barbing salon, restaurant, etc., in any African country, and see Nollywood programming on the screen. The popularity of Nollywood is also evidenced in its extensive and continuous coverage in local and international media, including CNN, Newsweek, BBC, Wharton@Work, etc. *Newsweek*, the American news magazine, even recommended the following ten movies for Nollywood fans: *Fifty, Diary of a Lagos Girl, 93 Days, Couple of Days, '76, Blood Sisters, Mr & Mrs, October 1, 30 Days in Atlanta* and *The Encounter*.[133]

---

131 *The Guardian* (Nigeria) Thursday, August 10, 2017.ps 43 We have produced more local content than we have ever done.

132 Ibid. – *The Guardian* Thursday, August 10, 2017. ps. 43.

133 http://www.newsweek.com/nollywood-10-films-see-413182 iROKOtv;

iROKOtv

Jason Njoku, the founder of Nollywoodlove, iROKOtv and the ROK Studios, is a pioneer in the digitisation of Nollywood and the expansion of the access and reach of Nollywood through digital and online platforms.

Though he is currently better-known for iROKOtv, his first digital and entrepreneurial creation was Nollywoodlove.[134] This was a YouTube channel founded in September 2010, but which, within one year of its launch, had close to 50 million views, with over 1.2 million views monthly. A measure of the interest in Nollywood was that viewership was from a global audience from over 230 countries and territories in the world. Even Njoku admitted that he was astounded by the sheer "scale and speed of Nollywood's success". Recognising its socio-cultural significance, he added that "Nollywood as a phenomenon has been one of most underappreciated social, cultural and economic movements coming out of Africa. I believe that Nollywood is Nigeria's national treasure – an amazing way to crystallise our culture, aspirations and attitudes today."

The success and reach of Nollywood has been achieved in spite of obvious existing challenges like piracy, poor production quality and infrastructure, lack of funding sources and venture capital, unreliable electricity, competition and disorder of an emerging market.

iROKOtv uses its online platform to distribute Nollywood content. To facilitate this, it has created and nurtured relationships and partnerships with film producers to acquire

---

134 Dipo Faloyin and Conor Gaffey Hooray for Nollywood: 10 Must-See Films From Nigeria - Newsweek www.newsweek.com/nollywood-10-films-see

and create content. When movies are streamed online, the audience automatically becomes global.

The company also retained a large portfolio of over 5,000 films, along with 500,000 registered users. iROKOtv used a low-cost entry strategy, charging only $5 per month for subscription to enable users watch unlimited Nollywood movies, without the distraction of advertisements. Jason Njoku also has iRoking. This provides digital access to Nigerian and West African music. iRoking has music from over 200 artistes.[135]

The launch of iROKOtv, a proprietary video-on-demand service, in December 2011, migrated viewers to a subscription-based access to its bouquet of movies. Within 18 months, i.e., mid-2013, iROKOtv was already generating over 50% revenue for the company while YouTube generated below 15%. This initial impetus emboldened the company to move to a subscription-only viewing business model and stop its free-viewing advertisement model in 140 countries where it hitherto generated revenues in April 2014.[136] In about one year, from early 2014 to early 2015, fee-paying subscribers in Africa had grown from 2% to 11%, representing 450% year-on-year growth, and Nigeria contributed the fastest growth category.

For a business to willingly shrink its customer base and move up in the revenue ladder to a smaller but higher-paying customer

135 For more on Nollywoodlove, read *Nigerian Internet Entrepreneur Takes Nollywood To The World* - Mfonobong Nsehe https://www.forbes.com/sites/mfonobongnsehe/2011/08/16/nigerian-internet-tycoon-takes-nollywood-to-the-world/3/#f4f2072595d0 Aug 16, 2011.
136 Nollywood 2.0: how tech is making Africa's movie industry a global leader http://ventureburn.com/2012/11/nollywood-2-0-how-tech-is-making-africas-movie-industry-a-global-leader/ By Victoria Soroczynski on 12 November, 2012

category is indicative of its confidence in the opportunities inherent in this customer category. Soon enough, this bet began to pay off for iROKOtv.

Greater evidence of growth opportunities in the sector and its capacity to reach a larger percentage of interested publics was the company's decision to initiate a process of forward and backward integration. From NollywoodTV on YouTube, to iROKOtv, the company expanded to ROK Studios in October 2014, to finance and produce Nollywood movies, with the expectation to improve the quality of Nollywood films and also produce 200 movies in-house. It also has its own app and has launched its internet kiosks across parts of Lagos, where subscribers of iROKOtv can freely download data and watch Nollywood movies.[137] Taking it further, in 2018, ROK TV launched two TV channels on DSTV and GOTV, expanding satellite television access of Nollywood and other African movies in many parts of Africa.

Nollywood and Hollywood

Another measure of the success of Nollywood is the growing interest in and participation of Hollywood actors and stars in Nollywood movies. Examples are Vivica Fox in *Black Gold* (2011) and Thandie Newton in *Half of a Yellow Sun (2013)*.

Half of A Yellow Sun marked a shift in the financing and production of movies in Nigeria. With an experienced cast of Nigerian and international actors and actresses, including Chiwetel Ejiofor,

---

137 Ibid. Also, for additional information on the evolution of iROKO, see The untold Story of iROKO: How Nollywood's Digital Pioneer has Evolved to Embrace Consumers in Africa - Emeka Ajene . Published January 19, 2017 http:// venturesafrica.com/the-untold-story-of-iroko.

the lead actor in the globally acclaimed *12 Years a Slave*, and produced on a relatively high budget, it focused on quality production and sought a wider global market. Amongst many factors, its limited commercial success was evidence of the lack of readiness of the market to pay for high-budget movies. This may also have highlighted the impact of piracy in the marketing and sale of movies in Nigeria.

Nollywood – Local Affinity, Global Impact

Nollywood is currently a dominant pan-African socio-cultural integrative mechanism in the world. In West, Central, East, North and Southern Africa, Nollywood movies are shown on television channels. In Francophone Africa for instance, there is Nollywood TV with voice-overs in French. In many African countries, Nollywood films are translated into local languages – Hausa, Yoruba, Igbo, Kikuyu, Lingala, Swahili and several others. It was in Abidjan, in 2017, that I first ran into Nollywood TV, with all the movies voiced over in French. In Kenya it is shown on KTN (Kenya Television Network) and some other local channels.

A striking and recurring theme in Nollywood is that it has given over one billion people of African descent, all over the world, representation and a truer reflection of themselves in the global community. It has also established a sense of community, association and familiarity, as the films tell their stories. In essence, it has also given an audible, even, loud voice to filmmaking in Africa. In my travels across Africa, the response to Nollywood is almost always the same everywhere – one of interest, familiarity, association and affinity.

Nollywood – Lifestyle Impact

The cultural impact of Nollywood is the received and growing interest in African fashion - fabrics, designs, patterns, hairstyles, etc. Though certainly not new, people are even more comfortable wearing African attires and making fashion statements at formal and ceremonial settings like offices, events, religious places of worship like churches, mosques, etc., more so in African countries where wearing such apparels on a regular basis to formal places was not previously common. Across Africa, there is increased interest and awareness of the names, lifestyles and stories of the popular actors. Men and women admire and readily adopt the fashion statements and hairstyles they see in Nollywood movies.

Nollywood has also spurred interest in the development of local movie industries in other African countries. An evolving dimension is the growing interest in Nollywood in Europe, Asia and the Americas. The popular Nollywood actors and actresses are stars in Africa and the diasporan African communities, and are the subject of attention and adulation. Nollywood has therefore been a profound validator of African socio-cultural values such as hard work and results, crime and punishment, fashion, physical appearance, respect for elders, importance of family, shared success, etc.

Ehiedu E.G. Iweriebor, a Nigerian scholar has described these practices as cultural nationalism.

Chimamanda Ngozi Adichie, the popular Nigerian writer, calls it "my fashion nationalism" or "project 'Wear Nigerian'". She describes the impact of Nigerian clothing on her lifestyle and how she contemplated wearing only Nigerian designers to public events. She has repeatedly worn Nigerian clothing to events like the Dior fashion show in Paris, the New York Times "Times Talks" conversation series; the American Academy of Arts and Letters induction, in New York; the Women in the World Summit, in New York, etc. – adding that this decision would support the value chain in the Nigerian fashion industry and attract more interest and patronage. She highlighted the positive impact of social media and online access, as these added "vigour and visibility" to the work of fashion designs and designers. She went on to describe Lagos, Nigeria's vibrant commercial city, as the "most stylish city in the world, where fashion is the one true democracy". For Chimamanda Adichie, this was a "personal and political statement", as it also "resisted the standard ideas and language of global – which is. . .western fashion".[138]

Such sentiments have become bolder, more widespread, common and globally recognised. A *New York Times* report affirms the positive view of the Nigerian fashion industry, stating that "Nigerian designers have gained international recognition with a style sense that is inherently cultural."[139]

The Economics of Nollywood

Beyond its impact as a solid source of entertainment, as well as a social and cultural expository to the world, the Nollywood phenomenon has also become a profound economic success.

---

138 "My Fashion Nationalism", by Ngozi Chimamanda Ngozi Adichie in *Financial Times* – Life & Arts October 20, 2017. https.www.ft.co.

139 As Nigerian Fashion Booms, Women Lead Its Coverage in https://www.nytimes. com/2018/11/04/business/media/nigerian-fashion-magazines-women.html   By Adenike Olanrewaju. Nov. 4, 2018.

Following the rebasing of the economy, the Nigerian economy became the largest economy in Africa with a GDP of $510 billion in 2014. Nollywood was a discernible contributor to the economy, with 1.3% share of the GDP. In that year, a total of 1,944 movies were produced in Nigeria. It is estimated that Nollywood employs over one million people working as actresses, actors, producers, engineers, scriptwriters, content creators, casting photographers, cinematographers, sound mixers, costume managers, make-up artists, managers, marketers, distributors, retailers, etc. The industry has also contributed to the regeneration of interest in cinema houses in Nigeria and other parts of Africa. Had there been greater availability of movie theatres, digital cinema screens and general screen infrastructure in Nigeria and most African countries, there would have been greater content production and a more rapid growth of the movie industry in the continent.

It is important to reiterate that the attractiveness of Nollywood as an entertainment platform, creating access to movies, telling the African story to millions of viewers in different parts of the world, is empowering. However, also critical is its emergence as a viable business opportunity for actors, producers, entrepreneurs, venture capitalists and financiers who, beyond entertainment, have realised its reach and transformative business impact. For instance, in January 2017, Skye9 launched its digital and entertainment business with a focus on "African movies by Africans to Africans, and by extension, the whole world, through digital content creativity and development" to address the African entertainment market.[140]

---

140 *This Day* (Lagos) Nigeria: "Skye9 Set to Drive Entertainment Industry With Digital Content" By Emma Okonji.

Nollywood - Diaspora Access

Given the affinity with Nollywood in Africa, it is important to assess the level of interest in Nollywood outside Africa, especially with the diaspora. In various discussions with friends and acquaintances living outside Africa, it became evident that Nollywood has significant followership in the diaspora. Many families request for DVDs and VCDs from visiting family members and friends; some also buy from shops abroad that retail the movies. Others watch online, on Netflix, YouTube and iROKOtv, etc.; and many others subscribe to television channels that air these movies. In an important initiative, and in recognition of the global acceptance of African movies, Netflix decided to begin ordering original series from Africa in 2019.[141] *Lionheart,* directed by Genevieve Nnaji, attracted positive reviews, and had its rights acquired by Netflix.

In the same vein, in 2019, it was announced that Canal+, the French media conglomerate, acquired iROKOtv's, ROK Studios. StarTimes, the Chinese pay TV operator, beyond listing Nollywood movies in its programming bouquet, had previously expressed interest in taking Nollywood movies to China. These initiatives will, undoubtedly, enhance and accelerate the creation and distribution of Nollywood content.

Increasingly, there are award ceremonies and film festivals that take place in the UK, France, US, Canada, etc., that showcase and celebrate the films and stars of Nollywood. Interestingly, the participation and audience at such events is diverse, with Africans, Americans, Europeans and Asians.

---

141 Netflix To Order African Original Series in 2019 https://variety.com/2018/tv/news/netflix-order-africa-original-series-2019

Chapter Seventeen

ENTERTAINMENT

Entertainment in Africa has diverse genres and a long uninterrupted history. Here, the focus will be on music.

Pop Culture

Growing up as a teenager in the 1980s and thereafter, American pop music and culture were the dominant social themes of interest, attention and affection for youth. Artistes like Michael Jackson, Diana Ross, Barry White, Luther Vandross, Anita Baker, Stevie Wonder, Lionel Richie, Ray Charles, Mariah Carey, Elton John, Madonna, Marvin Gaye, Aretha Franklin, Prince, Bruce Springsteen, Police, LL Cool J, Peter Tosh, Mary J. Blige, Aaron Neville, Phil Collins, Alexander O'Neal, ABBA, Tina Turner, R Kelly, Toni Braxton, and many others, were idolised in the music scene, and their music played at parties and events. Any time top artistes visited Africa, they were treated like royalty. American music and artistes also dominated the top 20 and top 10 pop and R&B charts on radio and TV shows. Some of the shows had rebroadcasts in many parts of

Africa. Thereafter, a new generation of artistes came up with enthusiastic followership, like Alicia Keys, Usher, Eminem, 50 Cent, Chris Brown, Drake, Jay Z, Rihanna, Beyonce, and many others.

Shifting Gears – Pan-African Music

African music has always been present and popular in the continent, and this acceptance was strongest in the communities, cities and countries of origin of the artistes and the genre of music. These artistes were also national icons and stars. However, in the 1990s, and more expansively at the turn of the century, African music began to spread and make an impactful presence on youths across the continent.

It is important to emphasise that Africa has always produced pan-continental and global music icons whose music and sounds criss-crossed the continent. They not only performed in different parts of the continent, but also to global audiences. These icons covered various genres of music: Fela Anikulapo-Kuti – Afrobeat; Hugh Masekela – jazz, Miriam Makeba – jazz, Afropop; Khaled Hadj Brahim, Youssou N'Dour – mbalax; Lucky Dube – reggae; Salif Keita, Manu Dibango – Makossa; E.T. Mensah – highlife, Angelique Kidjo – Afropop and diverse; Yvonne Chaka Chaka, Brenda Fassie – Afropop.

Fela Anikulapo-Kuti

Fela was an iconic musician whose genre of music, Afrobeat, expressed Afrocentric and strong political views and was heard beyond the shores of Nigeria, his home country. He was a leading musician in the 1970s and 1980s. He had several hit songs including, "Colonial Mentality", "Unknown Soldier", "Zombie", "Palaver", "Beast of No Nation", "Suffering and Smiling", "Shakara", and "Water No Get Enemy". He was very popular for his lyrics, his mastery of the saxophone, prodigious talent, the down-to-earth and, oftentimes, acerbic tone of his messages.

He operated from Kalakuta Republic, his free-wheeling headquarters, a place for music, dance, wine and many other things. He was eccentric. The nightclub where he performed was known as Afrika Shrine. Fela also wore colourful and bright clothing when performing. The height of his eccentricity was his marriage in 1978 to 27 women, some of them his dancers and songwriters. Fela's Kalakuta Republic was destroyed and burnt down by "Unknown Soldier".

Fela's music had a largely unifying theme across Nigeria, as it spoke to the realities and challenges of the masses. His firm opposition to social injustice, military rule and his widespread use of pidgin English facilitated access to and engagement with a large swathe of the population, irrespective of social status and gender. He formed a political party called Movement of the People (MOP), the platform under which he wanted to contest the presidential elections in Nigeria. MOP was, however, not registered and he could not contest the elections.

Across Africa, Fela's music was liked because the theme was familiar and palpable. He also performed during concerts in Europe and America and collaborated with global musicians. Fela's sons, Femi Kuti and Seun Anikulapo-Kuti, have turned out be successful and great musicians in their own rights. Though retaining the Afrobeat genre and the fight against social injustice, each has his personal focus, band and slant.

By the time he passed on in 1997, Fela had impacted millions of Africans around the globe. He was clearly a progenitor of the modern wave of African music stars, singing to audiences beyond their home countries.

The continuing resonance of his work and legacy is evident, so much so that almost twenty-one years after his passing, President Emmanuel Macron of France, on his first official visit to Nigeria as president, in July 2018, visited the New Afrika Shrine run by Fela's son Femi Kuti. While at the Shrine, he danced, drummed and sang. Asked why he visited the Afrika Shrine, Macron stated that it is an "iconic place. . . of African culture", adding: "I know the place and have some memories", having previously lived in Nigeria.[142]

Miriam Makeba

Miriam Makeba[143] was a leading African musician who was active for more than half a century. Her music was transcendental and attracted affection from her home country, South Africa, and internationally. Globally, she belonged to a select group of iconic female singers whose music had a generational impact. Her popular songs included "Pata Pata", "Malaika" and "The Click Song". She sang in English, Kiswahili and her native Xhosa. The love song, "Malaika", was from Tanzania. She toured extensively and collaborated with great musicians like Harry Belafonte. She also sang at the birthday party of then President J.F. Kennedy.

142 President Macron reveals why he visited Afrika Shrine by Ifreke inyang in Daily Post Nigeria http://dailypost.ng/2018/07/04/president-macron-reveals-visited-afrika-shrine/July 4, 2018

143 For more on the life and times of Miriam Makeba, see also the official website dedicated to her life's work- miriammakeba.co.za

She was very politically conscious, an activist who campaigned against apartheid and racism in South Africa, the country of her birth. She also testified against apartheid at the United Nations in 1963. A measure of her political activism was her marriage to Stokely Carmichael, a leader of the Black Panther movement, and her exile to Guinea, where she lived for some years. She was also naturalised as an Algerian in 1972, where she participated in the first edition of the Pan-African Festival in 1969. The Miriam Makeba Prize for Artistic Creativity[144] is awarded in her honour, in September every year in Algeria, to recognise creative artists from Africa.

Manu Dibango

Manu Dibango[145] is a living legend and prodigious talent who has recorded over 50 songs. He popularised the Makossa genre of music, using a fusion of African folk singing and energetic movements. The genre is popular in Cameroon, Congo, Gabon and other parts of Central and West Africa. Beyond Central and West Africa, Manu Dibango is recognised and respected globally for his music and more. An astute saxophonist, Manu was the first African to make the global top 40 ranking with his 1972 hit song "Soul Makossa". A measure of his musical longevity and staying power is that, in 2018, he celebrated 60 years of a remarkable music career. He performed in Côte d'Ivoire in January 2016, in Montparnasse in April 2017, and has formal engagements well into 2020.[146]

---

144 Algerian Press Service http://www.aps.dz/culture/62837-forum-des-createurs-africains-institutiondu-prix-miriam-makeba-de-la-creativite-artistique.

145 For more on the life and work of Manu Dibango, see also the official website on Manu Dibango – www.manudibango.net; Three Kilos of Coffee: An Authobigraphy. University of Chicago Press, etc.

146 Ibid.

I am honoured to have met Manu Dibango twice. First, in Douala, Cameroon, and then in Nairobi, Kenya on 1 May 2018, during the 5th Safaricom International Jazz Festival. The venue was jam-packed; with everyone mingling, moving and dancing. There were more than ten artistes and bands, mainly from Kenya, and one from South Africa, playing on that day. The artistes included James Gogosimo, Eddie Grey, Ulopa Ngoma, Jazzman, Mzee Ngala, Jacob Asiyo, Kavutha Asiyo Edward Parseen, Juma Tutu, Afroject, Chris Bittok, Nairobi Horns Band, Ghetto Classics, Shamsi Music, etc. And their renditions attracted warmth and excitement from the audience.

True to the hype, advertisement and promotion, Manu Dibango attracted the greatest attention, cheers, applause and respect. When he was announced, it was clear that a legend had arrived. Though his performance was the last act of the evening, the ovation, loud screams and renewed energy that reverberated in the entire arena showed that Manu was the man of the moment. The waiting crowd went ecstatic when he came to perform. On stage, and during performances, he remained energetic and ageless. I watched him intently and marvelled at how, at 85 years old, he could still lead and sway the crowd and command such stage presence. He led the orchestra and organised the songs, the singers and the saxophonists. I counted 12 people playing the saxophone at the same time, all responding to different songs, impulses and directives. The order, organisation and performance showed experience, confidence and gravitas. He sang and spoke in English, French and his native Douala. For him, the stage was his home. Seeing Manu perform at close quarters reinforced my belief that sustainable greatness, in every sphere of life, is earned even though it takes time.

Youssou N'Dour

Though he had been in music for a long time, and is one of the most successful African musicians of all time, my first encounter with Youssou N'Dour was through his rendition, along with Axelle Reds, of the enormously popular 1998 World Cup theme song, "La cour des grands". People wondered who the lanky singer with a mellifluous voice was. When I met him in Dakar, in 2016, I was impressed with Youssou N'Dour's focus, simplicity and diverse interests. While he looks easygoing with a gentle mien, his Mbalax music and songs in his native Wolof and French are lively, engaging and energetic. The songs provide deep insights, and promote Senegalese and African music and culture. I also marvelled as he described his different activities and roles in government, business, social work and music. In spite of his varied roles and artistic longevity of almost half a century, he has remained active with high-level performances across the world, with the release of a new album "History" in April 2019.

THE NEW WAVE OF MUSIC

Significantly, the tenor and direction of modern African music and artistes have, of recent, become increasingly pan-African in content and collaboration.

The current generation of African artistes target the continent as their audience and market, as a matter of right. There is also regular collaboration or *collabo* between artistes from different parts of the continent. The melody and tunes of their songs are also cross-border, as they are appreciated across countries.

Along the wave of Congolese, South African, Cameroonian, Ivoirien, and other music genres across Africa, Nigerian music of the 21st century has become the dominant streak among the youth and young at heart across Africa.

A new generation of successful Nigerian artists with a pan-African and international flair include Asa, D'Banj, P-Square, Davido, Wizkid, Flavour, Patoranking, Burna Boy, Tekno, KCEE, Phyno, Kiss Daniel, Mayorkun, Adekunle Gold, Iyanya, Naeto C, Tiwa Savage, Olamide, 2Face, Don Jazzy, Yemi Alade, Timaya, Tekno, Wande Coal, Dr Sid, Korede Bello, Reekado Banks and many more. These artists command respect and extensive followership across the continent and abroad. They are in high demand to perform in sold-out concerts in Nigeria, other parts of Africa, USA, UK, Canada, UAE (Dubai), Oman and other parts of Asia.

Within Africa, other artistes include Sauti Sol and Nyanshinksi from Kenya; Diamond Platnumz and Ali Kiba from Tanzania; Charlotte Dipanda, Daphne, Lady Ponce and X-Melaya from Cameroon; Chameleone and Eddy Kenzo from Uganda; Bobo D from Benin; Floby from Burkina Faso; Chef 187 and Slapdee from Zambia; Zonke from South Africa; Berita Khumalo from Zimbabwe; DJ Arafat from Côte d'Ivoire; Fally Ipupa from Congo DR; Sidiki Diabate from Mali; Mr Bow and MC Roger from Mozambique; and many more.

An important generation of music stars include Youssou N'Dour, Salif Keita, Lucky Dube, etc. In-country, there were names like Sunny Ade, Ebenezer Obey, Onyeka Onwenu, Dan Maraya, Richard Bona, Magic System, Patience Dabany, Oliver Mtukudzi, Petit Pays, Alpha Blondy, Awilo Longomba, Fally

Ipupa, Papa Wemba, Koffi Olomide, Rex Lawson, Oliver de Coque, Fuse ODG, Toumani Diabate, Bobby Benson, Victor Uwaifo, Angelique Kidjo, Sonny Okosun, Kris Okotie, Ras Kimono, Panam Percy Paul, Bongos Ikwue, Majek Fashek and Evi Edna Ogholi.

In Kenya,[147] there were musicians from different epochs, from Joseph Kamaru, Gabriel Omollo, Them Mushrooms, Five Alive and Kalamashaka in the 1980s, and up to the 1990s and thereafter, Ayub Ogada, E-Sir, Nameless and Amani, as well as others like Daudi Kabaka and Kelly Brown.

In addition to the quality and contemporary nature of their music, the Nigerian artistes have built collaborative relationships with several celebrity American and African artistes. These initiatives have also raised the profile and cross-border appeal of pan-African music. Instances of such collaboration include:[148]

- Davido ft Meek Mill
- Wizkid ft Drake on "Ojuelegba" (Remix)
- P-Square ft T.I. on "Ejeajo"
- 2face ft Bridget Kelly on "Let Somebody Love You"
- D'banj ft Snoop Dogg
- 2face ft R. Kelly

In recent times, there have also been strong continental collaborations and performances. They include:

- Diamond Platnumz – at different times – with Iyanya, Flavour, Davido, Kcee, and Waje

147 Down colourful memory lane in Kenyan music by SYLVANIA AMBANI in Daily Nation 18/05/2018. www.nation.co.ke
148 http://www.africamusiclaw.com/top-8-nigerian-american-music-collaborations-you-should-know/

- Charlotte Dipanda with Yemi Alade
- Sauti Sol with Burna Boy, and Tiwa Savage
- Chameleone with Eddy Kenzo
- Emma Nyra, Cynthia Morgan and Victoria Kimani
- Nyashinski with Sauti Sol

This surge has happened within the context of growing expenditure in entertainment and media in Nigeria, projected to reach $6.4 billion in 2021, with the internet becoming the largest market, valued at $4.6 billion in 2021, higher than TV and video projected at $1 billion and $722 million. Significantly, the internet will be decisive in democratising entertainment and media in Nigeria, and Africa as a whole.

It is very common to hear Nigerian music on numerous radio and television stations in different parts of the continent, at day and night clubs, in shops, offices, etc. I recall my experience in 2011, early one morning in my hotel room in Kampala. Suddenly, the song, "Yori Yori" by Bracket just wafted through the air. My surprise was actually the sheer availability and presence of music by Nigerian artistes.

Also, in the second half of 2017, I lived in Abidjan for some time. A major surprise during my stay was that I heard as much Nigerian music, if not more, in Abidjan as I usually hear in Lagos.

The genre was played in the cars, taxis, workplaces, etc. Nigerian music was readily available and widespread. In 2018, I moved to Nairobi, Kenya. The experience was the same. Nigerian music was played in homes, private and public events, and everywhere in Kenya and the rest of East Africa. It was also not uncommon to hear Nigerian music blaring from the ubiquitous *matatus* meandering through the streets of Nairobi. This musical trend was also prevalent in Uganda, Tanzania, Zambia, DRC, Mozambique and other parts of East and Southern Africa.

African music has respect beyond Africa. In the UK and the US, the presence of Nigerian music at gatherings, events and departmental stores is *also* palpable. I recall hearing Davido's songs on Power FM 105 and Hot FM 97.1 "Top 40" on a cold winter day in New York City in November 2018. Similarly, Chris Martin, a seven-time Grammy Award winner and lead singer of the rock band Coldplay expressed his delight in watching Wizkid "as a dream come true".[149]

Social Media and Music – A New Wave of Influence

Social media has, in the early 21st century, sprung a new wave of influence in music and entertainment, especially among the youth in Africa. In music specifically, social media has enhanced awareness of, interest in and reach of the artistes. The increased availability of the internet and social media on smartphones has created instant and widespread access to the music, daily activities and lifestyles of these artistes. Concomitantly, leading African artistes have become social icons, trendsetters and significant influencers in their various communities, countries and even beyond borders. In trying to assess their level of influence, I used some digital and social media parameters.

---

149 Watching Wizkid Perform is Dream Come True – Grammy Award Winner ColdPlay by Njideka Agbo in "The Guardian' December 6, 2018. https://www.guardian.ng/life/watching-wizkid-perform-is-a-dream-come-true-grammy-award-winner-coldplay.

Social Media Platforms

As a result of the migration of private, social and business activities online, social media platforms have become significant locations for interactions, relationships, gatherings, meetings, networking and business. Social media sites have become veritable communities where people reside, work and play. That also explains the massive business successes achieved by video-sharing, e-commerce sites and smartphone makers like Apple, Amazon, Samsung, Alibaba and the leading social media – Google, YouTube, Facebook, Snapchat, Instagram, Twitter, Reddit, Flickr and others.

Social Media Platform	Users	Period
Facebook	2.6b	Otr 1, 2020
Google	3.5b daily searches on Google	2019
Gmail	1.5b users of Gmail	2019
Android	2.5b	2019
YouTube	2b	2019
Whatsapp	2b	2020
Wechat	1.1b	2019
Instagram	1b	2019
Tiktok	800m	2020
Alibaba	755m	2019
LinkedIn	575m	2019
Pinterest	367m	Qtr 1, 2020
Snapchat	229m	Qtr 1, 2020

Review date: May 6, 2020.
Research from company websites, https://www.statista.com/statistics; https://www. cnbc.com/2019; https://gadgets.ndtv.com// www.theverge.com/2019/5/7//

Changing Lexicon

The lexicon of social interaction is also changing, with words taking new meaning in conversations and social discourse.

Familiar and emerging terms include users, connections, views, comments, shares, likes, dislikes, handle, followers; daily, weekly and monthly active users; post, tweet, chat, message, inbox, general chat, private chat, insights, impressions, hashtags, and others. Importantly, the new and evolving usage of some of these terms have no relationship with their standard or usual daily usage.

Social Media Stardom

In times past, artistes released their record albums via music labels and access was gotten through radio and TV. Today we have iTunes, Spotify and many more digital options to stream music. Due to the extensive availability of dissemination channels and access in many cities and countries, youth have easier access to the works and activities of artistes. Artistes globally have deployed social media to develop and nurture their brands and their businesses. New songs and important messages are released on their social media handles and sites to their fan base and followers. Social media has created the platform for songs to be listened to and musical videos to be watched and downloaded from every location. Invariably, people become influenced by what they repeatedly hear and see. Artistes therefore monitor their social media profiles and seek to actively grow their social media connections, followership and interactions, which is then used to measure fan acceptance and progress. African artistes have utilized and deployed the medium effectively. Their songs are listened to and their videos watched all over the world. And since some artistes sing in African languages and shoot videos showing scenes, events and locations in their countries, they provide a direct window to their world.

Given their acceptance and influence, governments should leverage on the reach of the artistes and work with them to positively influence youths to communicate important social messages on education, healthcare, focus, hardwork, culture and heritage, etc.

Artiste	Song	Views on YouTube	Date Published
Davido	Fall	166,948,404	June 2, 2017
Davido	If	106,086,618	Feb 17, 2017
Davido	FIA	74,616,563	Nov 11, 2017
P-Square ft. Don Jazzy	Collabo	77,543,075	Feb 23, 2015
P-Square	Shekini	73,154,668	Nov 17, 2014
P-Square	Bank Alert	78,417,954	Sep 16, 2016
Wizkid ft. Drake	Come Closer	90,716,730	Apr 6, 2017
Wizkid	Ojuelegba	37,162,063	Jan 5, 2015
Wizkid	Show You The Money	28,899,888	Jul 16, 2014
Tekno Miles	Pana	125,461,234	Aug 22, 2016
Tekno Miles	Duro	71,885,341	Aug 13, 2015
Tekno Miles	Where	42,634,179	May 10, 2016
Runtown	Mad Over You	104,787,611	Dec 7, 2016
Runtown	For Life	49,249,990	May 23, 2017
Diamond Platnumz ft Mr Flavour	Nana	61,975,034	May 29, 2015
Diamond Platnumz ft. Davido	Number One Remix	40,817,717	Jan 6, 2014
Diamond Platnumz	Sikomi	41,574,694	Dec 5, 2017
Mr Eazi	Leg Over	65,052,572	Feb 10, 2017
Patoranking ft. Sarkodie	No Kissing Baby	42,922,466	Jun 27, 2016
Patoranking ft. Tiwa Savage	Girlie 'O' Remix	38,062,762	Feb 5, 2014
Patoranking ft. Diamond Platnumz	Love you Die	44,190,584	Sep 1, 2017

Flavour	Ada Ada	40,579,368	Jun 30, 2013
Flavour ft. Chidinma	Ololufe	37,074,240	Feb 10, 2015
Flavour	Baby Na Yoka	28,844,282	Jun 29, 2017
Tiwa Savage ft. Don Jazzy	Eminado	27,302,429	Nov 11, 2013
Tiwa Savage	All Over	39,706,274	Apr 13, 2017
D'Banj	Oliver Twist	52,218,828	Mar 19, 2012
Chidinma	Fallen in Love	72,509,735	Nov 16, 2016
Iyanya	Kukere	24,968,754	May 14, 2012
Mavins ft. Don Jazzy, Reekado Banks, Di'ja, Korede Bello	Adaobi	43,719,084	Oct 19, 2014
Mavins ft. Don Jazzy, Tiwa Savage, Dr SID, D'Prince, Reekado Banks, Korede Bello, Di'Ja	Dorobucci	36,155,025	Jul 23, 2014
Olamide	Bobo	23,073,612	May 7, 2015
Yemi Alade	Johnny	116,476,298	Mar 3, 2014
Yemi Alade ft. Selebobo	Na Gode	28,880,276	Nov 4, 2015
Burna Boy	Ye	80,018,705	Jan 26, 2018
Burna Boy	Gbona	38,929,068	Sep 27, 2018
Davido	Assurance	56,600,663	May 1, 2018
Sauti Sol ft. Patoranking	Melanin	19,086,508	Nov 20, 2017
Charlotte Dipanda	Elle n'a pas vu	15,525,479	Dec 5, 2014
Magic System	Premiere Gaou	8,167,687	Dec 17, 2006
DJ Arafat	Gbobolor	6,775,449	Mar 13, 2015
Daphne	Calée	24,165,422	Mar 30, 2017
Daphne	Jusqu'à La Gare	19,408,548	Nov 15, 2017
Koffi Olomide	Nyataquance	9,547,617	Mar 4, 2017
Awilo Longomba	Gate le coin	7,064,940	May 24, 2009
Fally Ipupa	Eloko Oyo	55,163,024	Apr 7, 2017

Fally Ipupa	Original	38,228,899	May 5, 2014
Fally Ipupa	Service	23,951,390	Sep 9, 2013
Nyashinski	Malaika	9,794,335	May 16, 2017
Nyashinski	Mungu Pekee	7,928,579	Oct 13, 2016
Nathaniel Bassey ft. Enitan Adaba	Imela (Thank You)	43,191,769	Sep 6, 2012
Sinach	Way Maker	149,159,996	Sep 6, 2012
Sinach	I Know Who I Am	74,284,174	Oct 7, 2015
Sinach	The Name of Jesus	46,193,449	Sep 12, 2015
Prospa Ochimana ft. Osinachi Nwachukwu	Ekwueme	34,928,284	Sep 10, 2017
Ntokozo Mbambo	Jehova Is Your Name	26,254,183	Dec 4, 2015
Jimmy D Psalmist	Mighty Man of War	43,034,527	Jul 6, 2017
Glowreeyah Braimah	Miracle Worker	3,679,542	Mar 9, 2016
Evans Ogboi	Onye	229,796	Jun 21, 2014

Review date: May 8, 2020.

Chapter Eighteen

SPORTS – A STRONG TWINE IN AFRICA

In all countries in Africa, sports is a major source of entertainment. Its influence permeates all spheres of life – lifestyle, social, government, politics, business and economic sectors, religion, etc. Where two or three men are gathered and engaged in a relaxed conversation outside family, work or money, the topic of discourse is almost likely to be sports. Also, while different sports are emphasised in different countries, soccer is generally regarded as *numero uno*.

Success in international sporting events provides relief and even stability for political office holders while consistent failure in sporting events attracts rebuke and vociferous criticism of sports administrators and political leaders, and this is used to measure performance in other, even unrelated, sectors. The influence of sports is therefore critical and defining. Towards the end of the 20th century, sports inexorably became an important platform for pan-African integration. This was manifested at several levels.

Following migrations of Africans to Europe, North America and other parts of the world, a lot of the young men and women got involved in many professions including sports, as they settled in their new home countries. They became involved, competing for places, not as foreigners or migrants, but as citizens and bonafide representatives of their adopted countries.

The Impact of Colonialism on Sports

Another dimension is the impact of, mainly, British, French and Portuguese colonial history in Africa, accounting for the presence of players with origins from former colonies in their national teams.

Sports as an integrative mechanism in Africa manifests in several sporting activities, but mainly in soccer and athletics.

Soccer

Soccer is a beloved sport of a large population of the world. Soccer evokes universal interest and followership. It even competes with American football in the US and Canada, rugby and cricket in India, Pakistan, New Zealand, Fiji, South Africa, Zimbabwe, Kenya, and others, and is being developed with huge interest and investments in China, India, Indonesia, Malaysia, in the Middle East, other Asian countries and other young footballing geographies. In countries and continents, soccer is played at national soccer leagues, with a defined number of soccer teams. The winning team gets a championship medal and financial rewards, while the top performing teams in the league qualify for continental league tournaments, like the African Winners' Cup, African Champions League, The European Champions

League, the Europa Cup, AFC Champions League, and others. Country national football associations also have tournaments where football teams battle to win cups. National winners also compete for regional and continental tournaments. At the country level, national football teams compete in sub-regional, continental and world championships like the African Cup of Nations, the European Nations Cup, Copa America, the Confederations Cup and the World Cup.

There is also a growing trend where, due to adequate funding, widespread television coverage and quality of games, interest in and followership of European soccer leagues have increased tremendously in recent years. The performance of players in the English Premiership, the Spanish La Liga, the French Championnat, the Italian Scudetto, the German Bundesliga, etc., are viewed and reviewed regularly by soccer fans across Africa. On the flip side, this has led to a decline in interest and followership of soccer teams and football leagues in different parts of Africa. While I grew up following the field exploits of teams like IICC Shooting Stars, Rangers International, Bendel Insurance, Standard, Raccah Rovers, Mighty Jets, Sharks, Red Devils, Alyufsalam Rocks, NNB, Gor Mahia, AFC Leopards, Kampala City Council, Canon Sportif, Union Douala, Tonnerre Kalara, Accra Hearts of Oak, Olympic Sports, Esperance, Al Ahly, Africa Sports, ASEC Mimosa, Police, JS Kabylie, Zamalek, Arab Contactors, Nkana Red Devils, and many others in different parts of Africa, today, many youth and soccer fans in Africa are not aware, and do not follow soccer teams or players in Africa. Even more critical is the low level of investment in sports and soccer, in many African countries.

The World Cup

The World Cup is a showcase tournament which elicits global followership and nationalist and patriotic sentiment. Countries seek participation in tournaments and friendly matches which are all aimed at preparing the teams, ascertaining weaknesses, fortifying defences, strengthening strike forces, and generally striving to leave a mark on this global football map. Beyond this, however, we see Africans playing for their countries, but also see players of African descent representing their adopted countries.

The great and mercurial Eusebio, originally from Mozambique, tormented football defences in Europe and the world, playing for Sporting Benfica of Lisbon for 15 years, and was the icon of the Portuguese national team. Known as the Black Panther, his exploits during the 1966 World Cup, where he emerged as the highest goal scorer, are legendary. His impact in the sporting annals of Mozambique, Portugal, Africa and Europe remain indelible.

Also, although their history is much longer, and most cannot trace their origins in Africa, Brazil and other soccer teams in South America also attract attention and support because of their football prowess, artistry and historical affinity.

An interesting aspect is that Africans support their national teams when they play at the World Cup and coalesce support for strong African teams. And where their country "representative" team is eliminated from the tournament, allegiance shifts to another African team. And it goes on and on. In the same vein, there is also strong followership and support for European teams playing good soccer with a strong contingent of African origin.

Internationalisation of Soccer

The World Cup is a strong exemplification of the internationalisation of national soccer. During the 1998 World Cup, the French national team, which ultimately emerged champions, was also a global team and consisted of players with varied and diverse historical backgrounds and some of African origins:[150]

i.   Marcel Desailly – Ghana.
ii.   Zinedine Zidane – Algeria
iii. Patrick Vieira – Senegal
iv.   Christian Karembeu – New Caledonia
v.   Thierry Henry – Martinique
vi.   Lilian Thuram – West Indies
vii. Bernard Lama – Guyana
viii. Bernard Diomede - Guadalupe
ix.   David Trezeguet – Argentina
x.   Youri Djorkaeff – Armenia
xi.   Alain Boghossian - Armenia
xii. Robert Pires- Portugal/ Spain.
xiii. Bixente Lizarazu – Spain
xiv. Fabien Barthez – Spain

---

150 See also *France and the 1998 World Cup: The National Impact of a World Sporting Event* by Hugh Dauncey, p52-53 Geoff Hare, eds Routledge 1999; https://www.nytimes.com/1998/07/13/sports/world-cup-98-france-s-day-of-soccer-glory-arrives-upset-of-brazil-in-world-cup.html; https://edition.cnn.com/2018/06/08/football/france-1998-world-cup-win-anniversary/index.html; https://www.history.com/this-day-in-history/france-beats-brazil-to-win-fifa-world-cup.

Similarly, during the 2006 World Cup championship finals in Germany, 14 out of the 22 players of the French team had African origins.[151]

The pattern has continued. In the 2018 World Cup in Russia, there was a strong quotient of immigrant players with African origins playing for many countries, including France, Portugal, England, Belgium, Switzerland and Sweden. The 2018 World Cup winning French team is representative of this phenomenon. The team had:[152]

i. Steve Mandanda - DR Congo

ii. Steven Nzonzi - DR Congo

iii. Presnel Kimpembe – Congo

iv. Blaise Matuidi - Angola

v. Djibril Sidibé – Mali

vi. N'Golo Kanté – Mali

vii. Samuel Umtiti – Cameroon

viii. Kylian Mbappé – Cameroon

ix. Paul Pogba- Guinea

x. Adil Rami – Morocco

xi. Corentin Tolisso – Togo

xii. Benjamin Mendy – Senegal

xiii. Ousmane Dembélé - Senegal/Mali/Mauritania/Nigeria

xiv. Nabil Fekir – Algeria

xv. Thomas Lemar – Guadalupe/Nigeria

xvi. Thomas Varane – Martinique

---

151 Julio Godoy in World Cup Shows Different Faces of Immigration ://www.ipsnews. net/2006/07/sport-world-cup-shows-different-faces-of-immigration

152 (114) See Fifa.com for the full team list of all the countries participating in the World Cup. See also *2018 World Cup: Meet France's World Cup Players With Deep African Roots* in https://www.modernghana.com/news.

Additional "International" Contingent

xvii. Alphonse Areola – Philippines

xviii. Antoine Griezmann – Germany/Portugal

Critically, in spite of their historical origins, they were playing passionately for France, and the *Les Bleus* celebrated their win for France in Paris and other parts of the country on their return from the World Cup.

The Belgian national soccer team[153] also had a strong African contingent with eight players in the 2018 World Cup squad.

i.   Vincent Kompany - DR Congo

ii.   Romelu Lukaku - DR Congo

iii.   Mousa Dembele - Mali

iv.   Marouane Fellaini - Morocco

v.   Youri Tielemans - DR Congo

vi.   Dedryck Boyata - DR Congo

vii.   Michy Batshuayi - DR Congo

viii. Nacer Chadli - Morocco.

An additional measure of the diversity of the Belgian national team is the multilingual ability of team members in several languages including, French, Flemish, English and others. In fact, Romelu Lukaku is known to speak six languages – English, French, Kiswahili, Dutch, Spanish and Portuguese – while Vincent Kompany speaks five languages.[154]

---

153 See Fifa.com for the full team list of all the countries participating in the World Cup. See also *2018 World Cup: Meet France's World Cup Players With Deep African Roots* in https://www.modernghana.com/news

154 How Belgian footballers speak to one another BBC in *The Standard* Kenya. July 5, 2018. p52

European Soccer Championships

The Euro Championship also attracts attention beyond the World Cup, Confederations Cup and Champions League. It has huge and abiding interest among soccer fans because of its global followership and the quality of the matches, teams and players during the tournament, who are not restricted to playing for their national teams, and who have a chance to showcase their talents and skills to a far-reaching and almost-global audience.

There is also an interesting trend where Africans also play soccer, not just in their home countries or in Europe, but increasingly in China, India, Malaysia and other Asian countries, and in soccer leagues of other African countries. In Nigeria the soccer migration wave started in 1984 when the legendary Stephen Keshi moved to ply his trade in Côte d'Ivoire with *Stade d'Abidjan,* and then *Africa Sports.* Several other players followed. Over time, the direction of soccer migration has also moved southwards with non-national players featuring for teams in South Africa, and northwards, for teams in Algeria, Morocco, Tunisia and Egypt. These countries have a history and culture of soccer and well-funded national soccer leagues, and their national teams have played at the World Cup several times.

It is quite interesting to note that six out of the 11 players of the French national soccer team which started the 2016 semi-final match against Germany were actually of African origin. The African contingent in the French team included:

  i.   Blaise Matuidi - Angola
  ii.   Paul Pogba - Guinea (Conakry)
  iii. Patrice Evra – Senegal

iv.   Ngolo Kante – Mali

v.   Moussa Sissoko – Mali

vi.   Steve Mandanda – DRC

vii. Eliaquim Mangala – DRC

viii. Adil Rami – Morocco

ix.   Samuel Umtiti – Cameroon

x.   Anthony Martial – West Indies

xi.   Bacary Sagna – Senegal

Even more intriguing is the fact that 37% of the players in both the French and Portuguese teams that played at the Euro 2016 finals were of African descent, consisting of 11 from France, and six from Portugal; and 12 out of the 24 teams at the tournament had at least one player of African descent.[155]

The Olympics

The Olympic Games is another global showcase event that brings together men and women at the peak of their sporting prowess from different parts of the world to compete, showcase their talents and win medals at the Games. During the 2016 Rio Olympics, there were over 11,200 athletes from 200 countries and territories competing in 200 sporting events. The hosting rights to the Olympics is usually awarded to a city, after a very competitive bid and several capacity reviews. It is a sporting event in which the host musters resources, time and capacity to excel. Even when Mo Farah, Somali-born middle-distance athlete, and Elizabeth Ohuruogu, amongst many others, were running and winning many medals for Britain at the Olympics

---

155 https://www.theguardian.com/football/2016/jul/09/france-portugal-colonial-history-african-flavour-euro-2016.

and World Championships, many saw and claimed them as African exports. It is also now common to see many African-born athletes competing for Qatar, Bahrain and other countries in the Middle East.

Though not a new phenomenon, this tendency is growing. Abderrahman Samba, originally from Mauritania, grew up in Saudi Arabia, but competed and won medals and glory for Qatar in the 400-metre hurdles, a sport in which his personal best time of 46.98 was, at that time, the second-best time ever – just one year after debuting in the sport.

At the 2012 London Olympics, Ethiopian-born Maryam Yusuf Jamal gave Bahrain its first Olympic medal, while at the Rio Olympics in 2016, two Kenyan-born athletes, Ruth Jebet and Eunice Jepkirui Kirwa, won gold and silver medals respectively for Bahrain. More intriguing is that, at the same Rio Olympics, while the Kenyan Olympic track and field team had 55 athletes representing Kenya, there were over 30 Kenyan-born athletes competing for other countries. While this trend of global sports mobility is not restricted to countries and regions, it presents a growth and competitive opportunity for sports men and women; it also represents a responsibility to governments and sports administrators to ensure that policies and structures are put in place to nurture and retain their best and prospective athletes and talents. [156]

---

156 Abderrahman Samba runs second-fastest 400m hurdles ever in https://olympics.nbcsports.com/2018/06/30/ abderrahman-samba-400-hurdles; see also https://www.arabianbusiness.com/bahraini-overtures-kenya-born-runners-attract-medals-controversy.

Olympic Heroism – Stephen Akhwari[157]

Olympic history is replete with stories of desire, sacrifice, determination, failures, as well as courage, success and glory. Yet, heroism walks on both divides, of wins and losses; of successes and failures. The story of John Stephen Akhwari represents a striking tale of Olympic heroism in Africa.

Born in 1938 in Mbulu in the Manyara region in northern Tanzania, John Stephen competed in the marathon in the 1968 Olympics when he was thirty years old. The Olympics was held in high altitude, in Mexico. This was a challenge, as the athletes had to train not just for their events, but to cope with the physiological demands of high altitude.

John Stephen Akhwari was selected to run the marathon at the Olympics for Tanzania. That was his first Olympics and he obviously wanted to do his best. Prior to that, he had competed in middle distance races at several athletics meets.

He ran in a competition in Kampala, Uganda, where he defeated Mamo Wolde, the Ethiopian who won the gold medal in the 1968 Olympics in Mexico. He had also won a silver medal at the World Athletics tournament in Athens, Greece and participated in the Commonwealth Games and other championships.

When the race began, John Stephen Akhwari and all the runners took off in expectation. He ran well and was in a good place. However, at about 19 kilometres, the runners began to jostle for positioning, and in the ensuing melee, and with muscle cramps, John Stephen Akhwari fell on the tracks, injured his knee and

---

157 I met John Stephen Akhwari in Dar es Salaam, on May 28, 2018. We had a very interesting and illumination discussion from 9p.m. till late into the night.

badly wounded his shoulder. Medical personnel treated him and advised him to withdraw from the race for fuller medical attention and recovery. But he wanted to continue the race. With his knees bandaged and in severe pain, he insisted on continuing the race and promised to run slowly. He was allowed to continue the race. Given the passage of time, the race track became empty and lonely. Night fell. But he persevered. More than one hour after the marathon had been won at two hours, 20 minutes and 26 seconds, Stephen Akhwari limped into the stadium, which by now was almost empty as most spectators had left. Honours had been shared. The medal award ceremony had ended. However, an announcement was made that a solitary runner was about to finish the race; the lights came on and the stadium erupted in cheers and joy as he struggled to the finish line at three hours, 25 minutes and 27 seconds. At the end, when asked by a journalist why he insisted on continuing the marathon in spite of his condition, he made a statement of courage, conviction and love for country, that "my country did not send me 5,000 miles to start a race, they sent me 5,000 miles to finish the race."

In losing, John Stephen Akhwari became a winner. He became a legend, a true human hero and a shining light on the relentlessness of the human spirit. His story is a lesson in the importance of starting and the significance of finishing. Fighting to finish, he created an unlikely contradiction. A winning loser, or losing winner, all at the same time.

On a warm night in May 2018, in Dar es Salaam, I sat with John Stephen Akhwari in his hotel. I thanked him for his resilience, for what he did for Tanzania and for Africa. I wanted him to share insights with my team in Tanzania. I wanted him to speak to them about passion, commitment and belief, about endurance and dignity. I wanted him to speak on courage and the significance of finishing strong. A month earlier, I had told them his inspirational story. I used his story to challenge and energise the team. They were excited and pleased to hear about his story. Most of them, all banking professionals, had not heard about him before. I was quite surprised. It became clear to me that national educational curricula and socialisation systems in Africa must leverage on existing, but unsung national heroes to build greater belief, confidence and pride in self and country. At over 80 years old, and half a century after his Olympic exploits, he still stood tall and straight. In our discussions, he was straightforward and simple. Meeting him reinforced my belief that *there is simplicity in greatness.*

Tanzania recognised John Stephen Akhwari and awarded him a National Hero Medal of Honour in 1983. He was also invited to the Olympic Games in Sydney in 2000 as a distinguished guest. Similarly, he served as a goodwill ambassador to the 2008 Olympic Games in Beijing.[158]

Olympic Heroism – Maria Mutola

Maria Mutola was a star athlete for Mozambique. Also known as Maputo Express during her running days, she defied all odds to become an Olympic heroine. Her sporting journey started

---

158 For additional information on the story of John Stephen Akhwari, see, along with others resources: "Legend of Tanzanian marathon runner Akhwari: Winning is not everything" by Roy Gachuhi in *Daily Nation*, 31st March 2018; "A lasting memory: Tanzanian runner" by Cui Xiaohuo *China Daily/The Olympian* in http://www.chinadaily.com.cn/ olympics/2008-01/11 http://gidabuday.blogspot.co.ke/2013/07/; john-stephen-akhwari-tanzania-s-olympic. "Akhwari: Tanzania 's Olympic legend, who is ignored at home but respected globally", by Wilhelm Gidabuday

when she was 15, and proved to be a legendary journey with longevity, as she competed in the 800 metres women's race at six Olympic games. In Atlanta, USA in the 1996 Olympics, she won a bronze medal and then crowned her work in the 2000 Olympics in Sydney, where she won gold medal.

Meeting Maria Mutola, the "Maputo Express", in person, was again a reminder of the simplicity of truly great people.

Chapter Nineteen

THE TEMPLE OF SUCCOUR

In Africa, the belief in God, or gods, the existence of a supernatural being or beings, both as guides and directors of human affairs, remains strong. This belief system in the supremacy of God is also widespread and prevalent in all parts of the continent. This belief has not been dulled by the passage of time, government enactments, modernisation, urbanisation, economic growth and income levels.

African religions, with different manifestations, have always existed in Africa as a part of the wholesome lifestyle of the people in different parts of the continent. While there was a belief in the supremacy of one God, or different gods responsible for different aspects of life, the practice of religion was expressed in different ways in different places.

Christianity and Islam also have a very long history in Africa. Orthodox Christianity has early roots in Egypt with the Coptic Orthodox Church, the Ethiopian Orthodox Church and others. In fact, it has been posited that Aksum, in present-day

Ethiopia, was one of the first places in the world to convert to Christianity, and by choice, not imposition. Even as early as AD 340, the Basilica of St Mary of Tsion was commissioned for construction by King Ezana,[159] confirming that the predominant expressions and denominations of Christianity were introduced into different parts of Africa at different times several centuries ago. Nonetheless, the Catholic, Anglican, Methodist, Baptist, Presbyterian, Lutheran and many other Orthodox churches remain present and widespread in Africa, with large networks of parishes and followership across many age categories and economic groups.

Some of the churches have also modernised their modes of worship, practices and social interventions to make them more attuned to present-day needs.

The church was also an integral part of colonialism. The impact was the demonisation, erosion and decimation of local religions and practices.

Rise of Global African Churches

This phenomenon represents the emergence of large, modern and professionally-run churches in several African countries, with strong local networks of parishes or branches and a large followership. Most of these churches are mainly focused on their countries of origin, with minimal interest in expanding abroad. While the presiding leader or General Overseer (or GO, for short) may conduct and participate in conventions and

---

159 A review of the book: Ethiopia: The Living Churches of an Ancient Kingdom written by Mary Anne Fitzgerald and reviewed by Mike Eldon in *The East African*. May 26-June 1, 2018.

programmes abroad, the overwhelming focus remains local. Some of these churches include ECWA, NKST, Qua Iboe, Celestial Church,[160] Church of the Lord and other Aladura churches in Nigeria; The Lord's Chosen Church led by Lazarus Muoka, TREM led by Bishop Mike Okonkwo, Salvation Ministries led by David Ibiyeomie, the International Central Gospel Church led by Otabil Mensah, in Ghana; Church of Christ in Nations (COCIN), Household of God International Ministries led by Chris Okotie, Throneroom Ministry led by Emmanuel Nuhu Kure, Christ Chapel Ministries led by Tunde Joda, Latter Rain Assembly led by Tunde Bakare, Assemblies of God Church, Apostolic Church, House on the Rock led by Paul Adefarasin, This Present House led by Tony Rapu, HEKAN, Daystar Church led by Sam Adeyemi, Highlife Church led by Carlton Williams, Trinity House by Ituah Ighodalo, Christ Apostolic Church, CRC Christian Church, Bloemfontein and Doxa Deo Church, both in South Africa; Christ Is The Answer Ministries (CITAM), Kenya, and many others.

This recent phenomenon of the rise of global African churches has become a unique and interesting phenomenon since the late 20th century, but has accelerated in pace, size and fervour. In its broadest manifestation, the centres of global worship and spiritual succour are no longer just Rome, Jerusalem, London, and Mecca and Medina, but also in Nigeria and some

---

160 The Celestial Church and some others represent variants of large African churches as it has strong presence and followership mainly in Nigeria and Benin Republic, essentially due to its history and origins. Its founder, Samuel Bilewu Oschoffa was, though originally from Benin Republic, started and expanded the church in Nigeria, where the headquarters remains. Other churches have, though concentrated locally, also have minimal presence, parishes and expressions in other foreign territories.

other African countries. With declining fervour in Orthodox Christianity and worship in parts of Europe and North America, Nigerian churches have leaped forward.

Initially, Nigerian churches/preachers mainly participated actively in religious programmes, conventions and crusades abroad. However, the new wave involves the set-up and widespread presence of African, mainly Nigerian churches in the Americas, Europe and Asia, though with the spiritual head offices in Nigeria. The growth and rapid expansion of these churches has also been facilitated by the use of television and digital media in ministration, messaging, outreach, advertising and branding.

The new wave of global churches emanating from Africa are of two variants. The first expression represents churches of African origin that started in Europe. These churches expanded and became influential in their host countries, but with minimal initial presence in Nigeria. Examples of these churches include Kingsway International Christian Church (KICC) in London, UK, led by Matthew Ashimolowo; Embassy of the Blessed Kingdom of God for All Nations in Kiev, Ukraine, led by Pastor Sunday Adelaja, and several others.

The second variant consists of churches that started in Nigeria, but which now have clear and stated ambitions to operate internationally, in other parts of Africa and the world. These churches now have hundreds of parishes in different parts of the world. Also significant is that these churches have established outlets not only in locations of familiarity, like in West Africa (due to proximity and cultural connections) or the UK (as a result of historical, mutual use of English language and colonial ties), or the US (due to the significant Nigerian diaspora population resident there), but have actively set up churches in Western, Eastern, Central and Southern Europe, as well as in Central, Eastern, Southern and Northern Africa. Beyond Africa, Europe and the US, churches with Nigerian origin now abound in South America and Asia. Even more surprising is the extent of acceptance, penetration and success achieved in these far-flung locations, with minimal or non-existent historical ties with Nigeria. At a time, the Embassy of the Blessed Kingdom of God for All Nations in Kiev, Ukraine was the largest church in Ukraine and Eastern Europe. Significantly, most of its members were Ukrainians. In Istanbul, Turkey, and Dubai, the UAE, there are several denominations of Nigerian churches. These churches also have presence in other parts of the Middle East, Indonesia, Malaysia, Singapore, India and China. In Nairobi, Kenya, in April 2013, Living Faith Church, a.k.a. Winners Chapel, opened the largest church auditorium in East Africa.

Language has also not been a barrier as the churches have established strong and growing presence in Francophone and Lusophone countries. The churches are present in all countries in Francophone West and Central Africa, as well as in Portuguese-speaking Mozambique and Angola. There are Redeemed churches in Luanda, Angola and Maputo, Mozambique. I also saw a branch of Mountain of Fire Ministries (MFM) in Maputo. In one sense, the presence of the churches in these locations have been facilitated by the strong mobility tendency of Nigerian entrepreneurs, investors, traders, students and professionals. However, this has proceeded in tandem with the acceptance, attendance and integration of these churches in the foreign, host communities.

Unwittingly, the global African churches have made Nigeria a new global centre of pilgrimage and religious worship and a home of succour where people seek solutions for perceived mundane, and even intractable, personal, health and financial problems.

The Role of the African Church in Society

The Church in Africa has moved beyond proselytisation, evangelisation, winning souls and waiting patiently for the rapture, and has increasingly taken active roles in confronting and addressing present-day life challenges in the society. In this way, the Church complements governments' provision of social services, as a lot of people depend on the Church for solutions to unemployment, healthcare, communal water services and other socio-economic challenges. In some cases where the government is distant and the impact of the state is not felt, the Church and other religious and social organisations supplant the role of the state and provide essential services.

Education

The Orthodox Church – Catholic, Anglican, Baptist, Methodist – have always supported education. In this regard, the churches opened and ran several missionary schools. These schools were integral parts of the educational system during the colonial and post-colonial periods, as they provided quality education at affordable cost. The schools also provided the platform for the churches to disseminate the ethos and values of the church. The schools were reputable and had Christians of different denominations, Muslims and adherents of other faiths as students. In reality, a sizeable number of the post-colonial elites in many African countries went to missionary schools. In more contemporary times, the Church in Africa has opened a number of schools at the primary, secondary and tertiary levels. Today, some of the largest, modern, and most successful private universities in Nigeria are owned and run by churches. In fact, out of the 162[161] universities in Nigeria as at May 2018, 74 are private universities, out of which 33 are run by churches, representing 45% of the total number of private or non-state-owned universities. Examples include Covenant University, Otta and Landmark University, Omu-Aran run by Living Faith Ministries; Babcock University, run by the Seventh-day Adventist Church; Redeemers University, run by the Redeemed Church; Kings University, run by KICC; Mountain Top University, run by Mountain of Fire Ministries; Bowen University, run by the Baptist Church; Madonna and Tansian Universities, run by the Catholic Church; Benson Idahosa University, run by Church of God Mission; Anchor University, run by Deeper Life Ministries; Ajayi Crowther University, run by the Anglican Church; and many more – in addition to the primary and secondary schools and other tertiary institutions run by these churches.

In spite of the number of universities run by churches, questions have been raised about access to these universities, as their fees and charges are regarded as more commercial than charitable and missionary. The churches have, in response, explained that the provision of quality education requires significant investment and funding. For Africa, a balance is required. While quality education must not be compromised, it is important for governments, non-governmental organisations, religious

---

161 http://nuc.edu.ng/nigerian-univerisities/state-univerisity/.

organisations and private sector providers of education to focus on quality and affordable education, given the population, growing requirements, concomitant opportunity and the countries' need for impact.

Healthcare

Also, churches have built, funded and run many hospitals, clinics and medical facilities. Beyond these common themes, churches like Highlife Church have medical support and outreach programmes. Led by Pastor Carlton Babatunde Williams, the initiative *Lifeblood* creates awareness and engages in blood donation drives and encourages its church members and other citizens to voluntarily donate blood on a regular basis to facilitate the availability and use of safe blood by hospitals and medical institutions. This is based on its assessment that "every twenty-four hours, doctors in Nigeria need to find 4,863 units of blood for transfusions. . . to save the lives of sick children, sickle cell anaemia patients, women suffering pre- and post-natal severe blood loss, trauma victims, cancer patients and people with bleeding disorders."[162]

This Present House, Lagos, has been extensively involved in the rehabilitation of drug addicts. Run by Pastor Tony Rapu, a medical doctor, the church has focused extensively on the treatment, rehabilitation and care of hardcore drug addicts living on the streets of Lagos. The programme entails visitation, outreach and immersion into areas where the abuse of drugs is rampant.

---

162 "why give blood" in http://www.lifebloodnigeria.org; Blood banks and blood donations are important to national health. See also Running low: The story of Kenya's blood bank in Daily Nation, June 12, 2018. Page 4-5

These initiatives, led by churches, are widespread in different parts of the country.

Global African Churches

The Redeemed Christian Church of God[163]

Redeemed, as it is widely known, though modern in outlook and orientation, is actually not a young church. It was established in 1952, as an offshoot of the Glory of God House Fellowship in Ebute Metta, in Lagos, Nigeria. From 1952 to the early 1980s, Redeemed Church remained modest in its focus and ambitions. This changed in 1981 when Pastor Enoch Adeboye became the head and general overseer and the church adopted a global focus and strategy. This strategy is clearly outlined in Redeemed's mission and vision statement where it boldly proclaims its vision to "plant churches within five minutes walking distance in every city and town of developing countries and within five minutes driving distance in every city and town of developed countries."[164] Such a mandate places a responsibility and an ambition on the church to have massive geographical coverage in a short period of time. In the pursuit of the goal, RCCG has become one of the most aggressive and expansionist churches in the world. From a parish network of about 40 parishes in 1980, the RCCG currently has over 2,000 parishes in Nigeria. Beyond Nigeria, the church has the world essentially covered, operating in all continents and in about 198

---

163 http://www.rccg.org.
164 http://rccg.org/who-we-are/mission-and-vision/.

countries.[165] In Africa, the Redeemed Church is present in all geographic regions of the continent.

Quite astounding is the fact that in the US, Redeemed Church already has close to 800 parishes, with over 15,000 members in all parts of the country, yet its ambitions remain even greater. The North American head of the church, Pastor Fadele captures the plan this way: "At Redeemed we want to plant churches like Starbucks."[166]

The church has built its North American headquarters in Floyd, Dallas, covering 700 acres on which the following facilities are being built – a 10,000 capacity auditorium, a sports complex, a golf course and a university.[167] The centre, which cost $15.5m, is also called Redemption Camp, like its forebear in Nigeria. The plan is to make the camp a thriving community, with over 100 homes, schools, a community centre, a university, a fish farm and other projects. The camp, which already has "office suites, concert-style speakers and stage lighting, will be used year-round for a series of church events and made available for rental."[168]

I can personally relate with this drive because in early 2010, I attended an executive programme at Wharton Business School, in Philadelphia, USA. On a very cold snowy Sunday morning in February 2010, I was looking for a church to attend, so I

---

165 The thrills and frills of Redeemed Church's 2017 Congress in https://www.premiumtimesng.com/features-and-interviews/252765-feature-thrills-frills-redeemed-churchs-2017-congress.html.

166 The Redeemed Church of God preaches the gospel in US By Jason Margolis. BBC.com February 12, 2014 http://www.bbc.com/news/magazine-25988151.

167 ibid.

168 ibid.

searched the internet. I found a Redeemed Church parish, a walking distance away from Wharton, which I attended. Even then, the fervour was fever pitch, the energy level was high, characterised by prayers, praise and worship and other spiritual manifestations. The church also has an African Missions Organisation, a radio station, a TV station for its evangelisation programme and two livestream events, as appropriate, a leadership academy, and a virtual learning centre.

The Holy Ghost Service is the massive monthly outreach platform of Redeemed Church that takes place on the first Friday of every month, and draws attention and participation from all over Nigeria and other countries. It also attracts economic and political leaders, including heads of state and governments officials at different levels. Prof Yemi Osinbajo, Nigeria's vice president, was a pastor of Redeemed Church. A further manifestation of the sheer scale of the Church's ambition is the plan to build what would be the largest church auditorium in the world. At the 61st Annual Convention of the Church held at the Redemption Camp in August 2013, in Nigeria, the General Overseer, Pastor E.A. Adeboye, announced an audacious plan to build a three-kilometre long and wide auditorium, stating that the existing auditorium built in 2000, with a capacity to accommodate one million worshippers at a time, had become too small for the requirements of the church.[169]

---

169 RCCG to build 3-km long auditorium August 10, 2013. www.vanguardngr.com.

Living Faith Church

Living Faith Church[170] is also known as Winners Chapel, and at times, by the location of its headquarters, Faith Tabernacle or Canaanland, in Otta, Ogun State, Nigeria. Living Faith was founded in 1983 by David Oyedepo and has since expanded to other parts of Africa as well as North America, Europe and Asia. Even its official name, Living Faith Church Worldwide is reflective of its global interests and ambitions.

According to its president David Oyedepo, as at December 2014, Living Faith had six million members in 147 countries in the world.[171]

Shiloh

The church headquarters at Canaanland, Otta, is acclaimed to be the single largest auditorium in the world. The auditorium, which was opened in 1999, has a seating capacity of over 50,000, and an overflow of over 200,000, and is also used for weekly services. It is also the host venue for Shiloh, the annual gathering of the church's members and non-members, professionals, businessmen, journalists and government leaders from all over the world, in December every year. Shiloh began when the auditorium was opened in 1999. The programme is streamed live and watched all over the world.

---

170 For history, background, church activities and operations of Living Faith Worldwide, see www.faithtabernacle.org.ng.

171 https://www.vanguardngr.com Winners Chapel has six million members spread across 147 countries.

Education

One area where Living Faith is striving to leave a legacy is education. The church has opened schools across various levels of education – primary, high school and university. Living Faith Church and Pastor Oyedepo have midwifed three universities – Covenant University, Otta; Landmark University, Omu-Aran; and Crown University, Calabar. Oyedepo has also stated that the plan is to have a university in each of the six geopolitical zones of Nigeria.

Covenant University desires to be a "world-class Christian Mission University, committed to raising a new generation of leaders in all fields of human endeavour." The institution is one of the leading universities in Nigeria, and operates a bold programme titled Vision 10:2022 in which it aims to be among the top 10 universities in the world by 2022, when the university will be 20 years old. The institution also focuses on research. The university's vice chancellor, Prof. A.A.A. Atayero reported that in 2016, the school had 13.7% of the total publications in engineering, 21.4% in computer science, 22.1% in business management and accounting publications, and 26% of all publications in Scopus for Nigeria in 2016.[172]

Furthermore, in a ranking of all Nigerian universities released in December 2017, Covenant University was ranked as the number one private university and number one in overall ranking for all universities.[173]

---

172 www.m.covenantuniversity.edu.ng
173 http://www.dailypost.ng December 17, 2017, Ahmadu Bello University as No 1 University in Nigeria by Fikayo Olowolagba

The church has also opened Kingdom Heritage Schools in Nigeria and other parts of the world.

The Synagogue, Church of All Nations[174]

The Synagogue Church of All Nations (SCOAN) is another well-known church in Africa. Led by Prophet T.B. Joshua, and based in Ikotun-Egbe in Lagos, Synagogue Church has become a major pilgrimage centre, attracting worshippers, not only from Nigeria, but also from different parts of Africa. Interestingly, Synagogue has strong representation and followership in Asia with people from Indonesia, Malaysia, Singapore, the Middle East and other countries in the region. Synagogue has some distinguishing features. Though not a fiery preacher in the mould of many Nigerian Pentecostal preachers, T.B. Joshua's style has been very effective in creating a platform for religious integration in Africa.

Unusually, for a large church, Synagogue does not have a large network of parishes or branches spread in Nigeria, or across the continent.

Media

The church has deployed its media resources effectively in creating access for church members and viewers across the world. Though other churches have media networks and TV stations, the Synagogue's Emmanuel TV with its wide-ranging global broadcast and coverage of the church activities, its philanthropy, its use of local and international television

---

174 See www.scoan.org, for information on the activities of Synagogue Church of All Nations.

anchors, and given the channel's widespread availability, has had phenomenal impact.

Social Media

The church also has a very active social media presence with three million Facebook fans and a subscription of over 600,000 on YouTube, with its videos attracting over 240 million views. Synagogue has also stated that its TV outreach is the largest Christian television network in Africa. [175]

Faith Healing

The belief that individuals with major personal and health challenges like cancer, mental health issues, delayed childbirth, widowhood, unemployment and financial difficulties can be healed or resolved miraculously constitutes a significant part of the message and activities of Synagogue Church. A large number of adherents from abroad actually visit Nigeria and the Synagogue Church, in search of healing and cure for several ailments as well as physical, spiritual and mental nourishment.

I vividly recall a Kenya Airways flight that I took from Lagos to Nairobi, in May 2018, and observed that over half of the passengers on the flight came from Synagogue and were returning home from a church programme. They all wore green t-shirts, all emblazoned with "Synagogue Church". I have also experienced these adherents on these pilgrimage visits in different African cities.

---

175 See www.scoan.org, for information on the activities of Synagogue Church of All Nations.

Presidential Visits

To attest to the fact that human problems have no age, race, resource or even positional barrier, several important dignitaries also routinely visit the church to deal with health and other challenges. Examples of presidential visits include those of Frederick Chiluba, the then president of Zambia; James Atta Mills, the then President of Ghana, and his vice president, John Mahama; Omar Bongo of Gabon; Joyce Banda and Bingu wa Mutharika of Malawi; Morgan Tsvangirai, former prime minister of Zimbabwe; and other political leaders like Winnie Mandela.

Another recent breed of presidential visitors are contestants for high electoral offices in various countries. In 2017, George Weah worshipped at the Synagogue Church, as a contestant during the presidential election, and also after his swearing-in as President of Liberia. It was also stated that T.B. Joshua encouraged President John Magufuli of Tanzania to contest the presidential elections when he visited the Synagogue Church. The case in Tanzania was quite interesting as both the then outgoing president Jakaya Kikwete, the newly elected President John Magufuli and the former Prime Minister Edward Lowassa, the opposition leader in the keenly contested election, had visited Synagogue Church at different times and were on hand to welcome him to Tanzania. Clearly, this represents a measure of comfort with the church, its leadership, and practices. The church also highlights and showcases these august visitors in its media outreach activities.[176]

---

176 For a snapshot on the TB Joshua's engagements in Tanzania, see. T.B. Joshua visits Tanzania. http://www.tanzaniatoday.co.tz/news/prophet-tb-joshua-visits-tanzania

Another aspect of the presidential engagement is the visit by Prophet T.B. Joshua to countries where he is received as a special guest and honoured by the presidents of the countries. In fact, during his visit to Tanzania in 2015 for the inauguration of the new president, he was received at the airport by John Magufuli, on arrival. In November 2017, he visited Colombia and met with President Danilo Recibe. During his visit, he held an open air crusade at the stadium, which attracted a large number of people. Interestingly, the country was inundated with tourists during that period who were in the country to participate in the programme.[177]

Building Collapse

In September 2014, a six-storey building under construction within the premises of Synagogue Church collapsed. In the unfortunate tragedy, 116 persons were killed, including 85 South Africans.[178] The tragedy and the associated loss of lives shook the foundations of the church in Nigeria and other countries.

Air Travel and Religious Tourism

Interestingly, though I had always known of the existence and location of Synagogue Church in Lagos, Nigeria, my first realisation of its international presence and impact was in the course of travels within Africa where people randomly inquired from me about T.B. Joshua and Synagogue Church and how to visit Nigeria for the church programmes or how to accompany

---

177 Tourists besiege Dominican Republic as TB Joshua holds 2-day crusade - Kehinde Oyetimi Nigerian Tribune November 27, 2017.

178 https://www.thecable.ng/many-dead-injured-in-synagogue-church-collapse.

a family member with health challenges. I also met people from West, Central, East and Southern Africa who had been to Nigeria or were planning to do so to meet with T.B. Joshua. I recall a particular case, on a flight on Air Nigeria from Douala to Lagos, where it was difficult to get seats as flights were overbooked. I was put on inquiry and asked some questions and realised that the deluge in passenger traffic was due to a church programme taking place at Synagogue Church in Nigeria, in which large delegations from Cameroon and other parts of Central Africa were participating. To further elucidate on the impact of the Church on religious tourism, T.B. Joshua in an interview, stated that the church is "Nigeria's biggest tourist attraction and the most visited destination by religious tourists in West Africa",[179] adding that immigration data indicates that 60% of foreign visitors into Nigeria are actually visiting Synagogue Church and that this has led to increased air traffic between Lagos and other parts of Africa.[180]

---

179 How My Ministry is Boosting Tourism in Africa, January 19, 2018 http://www. thisdaylive.com/index.php/2018/01/19/how-my-ministry-is-boosting tourism-in-africa.

180 Ibid.

Chapter Twenty

BRINGING IT ALL TOGETHER

Mind. Money. Matter: Pan-African Integration in the 21st Century is a testament to the evolution and direction of modern-day economic, social and cultural integration across Africa. In the 21st century, pan-African integration has moved beyond podia, parliaments, lecterns, soap boxes, summits and retreats. It has journeyed beyond presidents, prime ministers and other government officials in hallowed halls and revered chambers. It is no longer the stuff of legends of the 19th and 20th centuries. Yes, it recognises and appreciates the pioneering works of pan-Africanist heroes like Kwame Nkrumah, Julius Nyerere, Gamal Abdel Nasser, Léopold Sédar Senghor, Jomo Kenyatta, Jaramogi Oginga Odinga, Kenneth Kaunda, Eduardo Mondlane, Samora Machel, Ahmed Sékou Touré, Nnamdi Azikiwe, Patrice Lumumba, Haile Selassie, Habib Bourguiba, Tafawa Balewa, William Tubman and many others, but the generations of the 21st century have swung into action.

The Generation 21C is acting out and executing pan-African integration. This generation is pragmatic, rather than philosophical. They *do* pan-African integration. While the initiatives and activities undertaken may not have clear and documented philosophical and ideological foundations, they take action anyway. Interestingly, most of the economic, social, and cultural actors and purveyors of pan-African integration of the 21st century did not set out on such a grand mission. In fact, many of them do not realise the implications and outcomes of their actions. For many economic operators, it has been a fortuitous coalescing of plans, actions and realities. What many have done upon realising the long-term implications of their actions is to latch in on it, refine their vision and mission statements with Africa and Africans as the centrepiece. In essence, it is a catch-up with reality.

Mind, money and matter, in broad usage, represents the daily and current manifestation of African integration. First the *mind* is one of the most powerful resources of the human. It initiates, drives and coordinates action. That's why, in its use, it has built up and brought down empires, kingdoms, governments and people. The keenness of the mind partly explains the continued relevance of television, social media, the internet, radio, newspapers, books, entertainment, movies, etc. NEST represents a playing field of the mind.

Money refers to the importance and indispensability of finance in socio-economic activities. Money, like it or not, is critical in vitalising education, urban and rural infrastructure, technology, social services, gender equality, diversity and inclusion, agriculture, healthcare, telecommunications, tourism and other appurtenances of modern-day living. Therefore, commercial banks, merchant banks, investment banks, mortgage banks, community banks, industrial banks, agricultural banks, microfinance institutions, insurance companies, stock exchanges and other financial institutions are critical arteries and conductors of the modern domestic and international economy.

Matter represents industry, manufacturing, agriculture and the real factors of production. Matter facilitates the provision of infrastructure, and is represented in the book by entities like Dangote Industries, Comcraft Group and others. Therefore, the coming together of mind, money and matter is an expression of modern African integration.

Challenges Persist

In all, *Mind. Money. Matter: Pan-African Integration in the 21st Century* does not intend to create the impression that pan-African commercial, economic and governmental relationships are near perfect. Far from it. In fact, multi-dimensional challenges exist and even persist. There are frequent trade and political spats between neighbouring countries and trading partners. Even the regional economic communities, RECs, specifically created to facilitate economic and political integration, within the regional blocs, have been hamstrung by political bickering and the pursuit of national interests. My position, however, is that the vision, action and pace of pan-African integration in the 21st century has taken shape and is decidedly on course, because overall, it is the best course for all, both in the private sector and in government. More critically, it is proceeding because of, and in spite of, restrictions and challenges.

A Periscope for the Future

I see an acceleration of the outlined manifestations of integration in Africa. As the barriers to cross-border mobility are removed and there is freer movement of goods and capital within the continent, people will realise and take advantage of opportunities beyond borders. Firms will see their market as a community of over one billion consumers, rather than a nation of one million, ten million, or even 100 million consumers. This portends infinite possibilities.

Cross-Border Investments & Economic Activity

There is usually a heightened focus on the level of intra-African trade hovering at about 12%, but not much attention is paid to intra-African investments and industry. In addition to the banks – Standard Bank, FNB, UBA, Ecobank, Attijariwafa, Bank of Africa, Afriland First Bank, Equity, KCB, Zenith, GTB, Access Bank; and the telecommunication companies – MTN, Globacom, Airtel, Tigo, Vodacom, Maroc Telecom; and the conglomerates – Dangote, Comcraft, Mohamed Enterprises Tanzania Limited, Bakhresa, Lake Group, Arab Contractors; and other institutions with pan-African investments, more industrialists and investors will boldly explore and seize cross-border opportunities. In addition to these African Torchbearers investing and expanding operations in multiple African countries, another pattern exists where individuals invest in firms and entities cross-border through the stock exchange or even through private placements or share acquisition.

In April 2018, Tanzanian investors Aunali and Sajjad Rajabali acquired ten million shares of Safaricom, the Kenyan telecommunication giant, valued at KES 295 million, or about $2.95m.[181] Giving further vent to their commitment to cross-border investment in Africa, by September 2018, they had become the largest single individual investors in Safaricom by acquiring additional 11 million units of the shares valued at KES 277 millions, or about $2.77 million, taking their cumulative stock to 21 million units valued at KES 527 million or about $5.27 million, based on regulatory filings at the Nairobi Securities Exchange.[182] The duo had also invested KES 344 million in seven million shares of Equity Bank,[183] the regional bank from Kenya, with operations also in Uganda, Tanzania, South Sudan, DRC and Rwanda. In the same vein, following the decision by the government of Ethiopia in June 2018 to liberalise the ownership of some state-owned and state-run monopolies in the economy viz, MTN and VODACOM, both leading telecommunication companies from South Africa, immediately indicated interest in operating in Ethiopia.[184] These cross-border investment ventures will compel a robust and more accurate reporting and documentation of intra-African trade, industry, investments and economic activities. The role of the African Trade Insurance Agency, ATI, in providing political

---

181 Dar billionaires buy 10m Safaricom shares in *Daily Nation*. Kenya. June 11, 2018. P.2

182 Dar billionaires now top investors in Safaricom in Business Daily September 26, 2018. https://www.businessdailyafrica.com/news/Dar-billionaires-now-top-investors-in-Safaricom/539546-4778240-90c6e1/index.html

183 Tanzania billionaires buy Equity Bank stake in *Business Daily*. Kenya. June 8, 2018. P.9

184 South African Telcos say keen on 'attractive' Ethiopian market in *Business Daily*. Kenya. June 8, 2018. P.18

risk insurance, credit risk insurance, investment insurance and other risk mitigation solutions is important in supporting and facilitating intra-African trade and investments.[185]

Disintegrating Barriers

A growing and, perhaps, imperceptible hand in Africa is the slow but sure disintegration of linguistic, cultural, social, and economic barriers.

Language

Language barriers constitute a strong barrier to cross-border communication and interaction, at government, business, professional and individual levels. But my experience in the last decade traversing the continent has been that more people, including government leaders and other officials, business leaders, etc., are more willing to work with and accept individuals from other language groups. The resistance has reduced and openness has increased. This is not sentimental and emotional, but practical and realistic. In essence, political, social, and economic leaders see opportunity across the language aisle, and are willing to explore and make increased effort. There is a willingness to listen, hear and even attempt to speak another language.

I have personally seen this level of progress in Cameroon, Côte d'Ivoire, Angola, Mozambique, Benin, Burkina Faso, Senegal, Guinea, Congo, and DR Congo, Mali, Tchad and Gabon. In spite of the fact that English is not the primary language of

---

185 www.ati-aca.org

communication in these countries, there has been a clear effort to bridge the language barrier to ease communication. Countries that are officially bilingual in two main foreign languages, like Cameroon, Rwanda, and Burundi, have an advantage, as citizens can communicate in English and French. In fact, Rwanda has pushed the bar. Though initially, a French-speaking country, Rwanda, for all practical purposes, is quadrilingual with French, English, Kinyarwanda and Kiswahili spoken with ease in the country, in formal and informal settings, and as national languages. With English and French being the official language in most African countries; with Kiswahili widely spoken in East Africa and the Great Lakes region; and with Kinyarwanda being the national language, Rwandese citizens and officials are able to engage more easily across national, regional and language frontiers. In neighbouring Burundi, Kirundi, Kiswahili and French are also widely spoken. In Mozambique, though officially Portuguese-speaking, English is widely spoken in the country, in formal and informal settings.

A very positive development is the decision by the South African government in September 2018 to introduce Kiswahili as a second language of instruction in all public, private and independent schools in the country, effective 2020.[186] This will expand the reach and scope of the language and facilitate communication in East and Southern Africa.

Economics

Political and economic leaders in Africa are increasingly seeking investments and are willing to open doors and work with

---

186 Kiswahili now to be taught in all South African schools in The Guardian – Tanzania P1 September 18, 2018.

potential investors from other parts of the continent, and the world. They recognise the actual benefits of the investments in terms of economic activity, employment generation, payment of taxes, provision of infrastructure, social amenities, etc., and are willing to create the facilitative environment and grant concessions to attract significant investments.

Technology

I also see continuing rapid growth in the use and deployment of technology. Increasingly, digitalisation is enhancing economic integration in Africa. Mobile banking and mobile money have facilitated financial inclusion and the availability of financial services in-country. In a boost to financial inclusion in Uganda, 57% of the adult population use digital payment services, while 58% use formal financial services.[187] The next phase will be to accelerate cross-border deployment of the solution. In fact, over 40% of the Kenyan economy passes through M-Pesa, which is the predominant mobile money service, offered by Safaricom in Kenya. Overall, there are over 37 million mobile money accounts in the country which process approximately 130 million transactions i.e., between KES 290 billion and KES 320 billion, which is about $2.9 billion to $3.2 billion monthly, powered through Safaricom, Airtel and Telkom.[188] With a population of 50 million and a GDP of $100 billion, the mobile money impact in the economy is sizeable. Vodacom, the single largest shareholder in Safaricom, has made clear its intention to offer its flagship mobile money product beyond

---

187 FINSCOPE   UGANDA   http://fsduganda.or.ug/wp-content/uploads/2018/10/
   FinScope-Uganda-Survey-Report-2018.pdf p.23-27.

188 Tax hike on mobile money will hurt industry, says Safaricom, in *The Standard.*
   Kenya. June 18, 2018. P. 28

Kenya, Tanzania, Mozambique, DR Congo and Lesotho through which its 33.3 million mobile money users process R100 billion or about $7.43 billion transactions monthly to new markets in Africa.[189] Similarly, in a game-changing move, MTN and Orange, two leading telecom service providers in Africa, announced the launch of *Mowali*, a pan-African mobile money initiative that will enable over 100 million mobile money subscribers of both telecommunication companies in 22 countries to freely transact and transfer money within the *Mowali* network. It is interesting that both companies set aside competition and business rivalry to grow business, build an inclusive network and serve customers.[190] In July 2018, the Ethiopian government announced its discussions for Safaricom to provide M-pesa mobile services in Ethiopia.

Over time, I expect that this service will be integrated with the other mobile money initiatives in other economies in the region.

Also, Airtel, a leading telecommunications company, has a *One Network* structure and service whereby calls made by about 80 million subscribers on the Airtel network, in 15 African countries, are regarded as local calls and charged local rates whenever the calls are initiated and terminated on its network – irrespective of the caller's location. In other words, an Airtel subscriber in Congo Brazzaville calling an Airtel subscriber in Uganda is charged domestic call rates, even when the call is international.

---

189 Vodacom spreads its wings in **Businessday** South Africa www.businessday.co.za
190 Orange and MTN launch pan-African mobile money interoperability to scale up mobile financial services across Africa. www.orange.com

Furthermore, UBA's Connect Africa and Africash, as well as Ecobank's Rapid Transfer have strong remittance and funds transfer platforms that enable the movement of funds to beneficiaries across the continent, where the banks have operations.

There are also established and emerging electronic and financial payments and financial technology (Fintech) companies, with a pan-African interest, presence and focus. They include Interswitch[191], WeCashUp, Cellulant, Flutterwave, Paga, etc, which provide transaction processing, payment platforms technology integration, payment infrastructure and other solutions to public and private sector institutions in oil and gas, transportation, health, aviation, telecommunications, education and other sectors.

In the field of communication, there are many organisations in the electronic, print, and digital media, with country, regional, and pan-African coverage that provide information on events and activities across the continent. They include SABC, Africa 24, Arise TV, *New African, African Review, African News, Jeune Afrique*, allafrica.com, africawebtv, and many more. In education, there is an interesting, but emerging trend where a growing number of African students are pursuing higher education in other African countries.

On the whole, a key message of the book has been that pan-African integration is real and happening daily, without fanfare and speeches. It has become inexorable and unstoppable and is silently chipping away at established structures and boundaries. I expect that things will get better.

---

191 https://www.interswitchgroup.com

REFERENCES

Aarons, E., 'France's and Portugal's Colonial Heritage Brings African Flavor to Euro 2016', 9 July 2016, https://www.theguardian.com/football/2016/jul/09/france-portugal-colonial-history-african-flavour-euro-2016, (Accessed 7 October 2017).

Adepetun, A., 'Africa's Mobile Phone Penetration Now 67%', *The Guardian,* 17 June 2015, https://guardian.ng/technology/africas-mobile-phone-penetration-now-67/, (Accessed 26 June 2017).

Adichie, C. N., 'My Fashion Nationalism', *Financial Times*, 20 October 2017, https://www.ft.co, (Accessed 11 January 2018).

AFP, 'Benin Hit by Neighbouring Nigeria's Car Import Ban', *New Vision,* 29 January 2017, https://www.newvision.co.ug/new_vision/news/1445050/benin-hit-neighbouring-nigerias-car-import-ban, (Accessed 3 March 2018).

Ajene, E., 'The Untold Story of iROKO: How Nollywood's Digital Pioneer has Evolved to Embrace Consumers in Africa, Ventures Africa', 19 January 2017, http://venturesafrica.com/the-untold-story-of-iroko/

Akhwari, J. S., interviewed by Emeke Iweriebor, 2018, Dar es Salaam, Tanzania.

Ambani, S., 'Down Colourful Memory Lane in Kenyan Music', *Daily Nation,* 12 May 2018, https://www.nation.co.ke/lifestyle/showbiz/Down-colourful-memory-lane-in-Kenyan-music/1950810-4568212-hlqtxz/index.html, (Accessed 4 May 2018).

Baril, H., 'National Bank of Canada Purchases an Equity Stake in the African Financial Group NSIA', *National Bank,* 25 March 2015, https://www.marketwatch.com/press-release/national-bank-of-canada-purchases-an-equity-stake-in-the-african-financial-group-nsia-2015-03-25, (Accessed 8 May 2018).

Bavier J., 'Ivory Coast Government Approves Sale of Stake in NSIA Banque-CI', *Reuters,* 3 June 2016, https://www.reuters.com/article/ivorycoast-bank-idUSL8N18V3D0, (Accessed 7 July 2018).

BNP Paribas, *CEM, A Bank with Its Roots in the Textile and Engineering Industries,* https://history.bnpparibas/document/cem-a-bank-with-its-roots-in-the-textile-and-engineering-industries/, (Accessed 7 July 2018).

Chambre des Mines – Federation des Entreprises Du Congo, *DRC Mining Industry Annual Report,* 2015, http://congomines.org/system/attachments/assets/000/001/087/original/CdM_annual_Report_2015_EN_-_0402_2016.pdf?1455112232, (Accessed 8 February 2018).

Chandaria M., interviewed by Henry McGee, 2014, Baker Library Historical Collections, Harvard Business School, http://www.hbs.edu/creating-emerging-markets/, (Accessed 5 June 2017).

Chazingwa, M., 'Zambia: Kasumbalesa Upgraded, Proves Effective', *All Africa,* 21 October 2015, https://allafrica.com/stories/201510220168.html, (Accessed 3 April 2018).

Coffey, H., 'Ethopian Airplanes Operates First All-Female Flight Crew in Africa', 20 December 2017, https://www.independent.co.uk/travel/news-and-advice/ethiopian-airlines-all-female-flight-crew-pilots-addis-ababa-lagos-first-africa-a8120816.html, (Accessed 20 December 2017).

Dangote, A., 'The Story of the Dangote Group', *The Role of Business in Driving Sustainable Business Development,* Lagos, 2016.

Daniels, B., 'The Thrills and Frills of Redeemed Church's 2017 Congress', *Premium Times,* 18 December 2017, https://www.premiumtimesng.com/features-and-interviews/252765-feature-thrills-frills-redeemed-churchs-2017-congress.html, (Accessed 17 January 2018).

Dibango, M., *Three Kilos of Coffee: An Autobiography,* Chicago, University of Chicago Press, 1989.

Egene, G., 'Dangote Group Controls 43% of Nigerian Stock Market', *Thisday Newspapers*, 9 March 2016, https://www.thisdaylive.com/index.php/2016/03/09/dangote-group-controls-43-of-nigerian-stock-market/amp/, (Accessed 9 December 2017).

Eldon, M., 'New Tome: A Journey Through Ethiopian Churches', *The East African,* 1 June 2018, http://www.theeastafrican.co.ke/magazine/A-journey-through-Ethiopian-churches/434746-4580272-txichvz/index.html, (Accessed 12 June 2018).

Faloyin, D. and Gaffey, C., *Hooray for Nollywood: 10 Must-See Films from Nigeria,* 1 November 2016, https://www.

newsweek.com/nollywood-10-films-see-413182, (Accessed 14 February 2018).

Gacheru, M. W., 'Authors Trace Awori Dynasty to 18th Century Patriarch', *Business Daily Africa,* 3 May 2018, https://www.businessdailyafrica.com/lifestyle/books/Authors-trace-Awori-dynasty-to-18th-century-patriarch, (Accessed 30 May 2018).

Gachuhi, R., 'Legend of Tanzanian Marathon Runner Akhwari: Winning Is Not Everything', *Daily Nation*, 31 March 2018, https://www.nation.co.ke/sports/talkup/Legend-of-Tanzanian-marathon-runner-John-Stephen-Akhwari/441392-4365250-jyn3ek/index.html, (Accessed 24 May 2018).

George T., 'Many Dead, Injured in Synangogue Church Collapse', *The Cable,* 12 September 2014, https://www.thecable.ng/many-dead-injured-in-synagogue-church-collapse, (Accessed 6 February 2016).

Godoy, J., 'World Cup Shows Different Faces of Immigration', 12 July 2006, http://www.ipsnews.net/2006/07/sport-world-cup-shows-different-faces-of-immigration/, (Accessed 1 January 2018).

Grez, M., 'France's 'Rainbow Team' looks back at historic World Cup triumph', *CNN,* 6 July 2018, https://edition.cnn.com/2018/06/08/football/france-1998-world-cup-win-anniversary/index.html, (Accessed 12 July 2018).

Hare, G., 'France and the 1998 World Cup: The National Impact of a World Sporting Event', London, Routledge, 1999.

Hedley, N., 'Vodacom Spreads Its Wings to Reach New African Markets', *Business Day,* 10 May 2018, https://

www.businesslive.co.za/bd/companies/telecoms-and-technology/2018-05-10-vodacom-spreads-its-wings-to-reach-new-african-markets/, (Accessed 11 June 2018).

History, 'France Beats Brazil to Win FIFA World Cup', 16 November 2009, https://www.history.com/this-day-in-history/france-beats-brazil-to-win-fifa-world-cup, (Accessed 8 November 2017).

International Monetary Fund, *Letter of Intent, Memorandum of Economic and Financial Policies and Technical Memorandum of Understanding*, Ukraine, 2016, https://www.imf.org/external/np/loi/2016/ukr/090116.pdf, (Accessed 2 August 2018).

Inyang, I., 'President Macron Reveals Why He Visited Afrika Shrine', *Daily Post*, 4 July 2018, http://dailypost.ng/2018/07/04/president-macron-reveals-visited-afrika-shrine, (Accessed 7 August 2018).

Izuzu, C., '2016 Cannes Film Festival', 12 May 2016, https://www.pulse.ng/entertainment/movies/2016-cannes-film-festival-4-nigerian-films-screening-at-69th-edition-id5021752.html, (Accessed 8 November 2017).

Jacks, M., 'Nollywood Contributes Massively to Nigeria's GDP', 7 April 2014, http://venturesafrica.com/nollywood-contributes-massively-to-nigerias-gdp/, (Accessed 25 November 2017).

Jorgic, D., 'Kenya's Comcraft Group Discussing Possible Share Offerings-Chairman', 9 April 2014, https://www.reuters.com/article/us-africa-summit-comcraft/kenyas-comcraft-group-discussing-possible-share-offerings-chairman-idUSBREA380HY20140409, (Accessed 14 February 2018).

Jorgic, D. and Omulo, I., 'Bahraini Overtures to Kenya-

Born Runners Attract Medals, Controversy', *Lifestyle*, 17 August 2016, https://www.arabianbusiness.com/bahraini-overtures-kenya-born-runners-attract-medals-controversy-642770.html, (Accessed 18 September 2018).

Juma, V., 'Dar Billionaires Buys Safricom Shares', *Daily Nation,* 28 September 2018, https://www.businessdailyafrica.com/news/Dar-billionaires-now-top-investors-in-Safaricom/539546-4778240-90c6e1/index.html, (Accessed 29 September 2018).

Kelly, C., 'Liquid Telecom and Telecom Egypt to Complete pan-African Fibre Network', 16 July 2018, https://www.totaltele.com/500618/Liquid-Telecom-and-Telecom-Egypt-to-complete-pan-African-fibre-network, (Accessed 30 July 2018).

Kometa, R. K., 'Central Africa: CEMAC Zone – Circulation Is Free', 31 October 2017, https://allafrica.com/stories/201711010234.html, (Accessed 8 December 2017).

Konkobo, L., 'Fespaco 2017: Six Things about Africa's Biggest Film Festival', *BBC,* 3 March 2017, https://www.bbc.com/news/world-africa-39133258, (Accessed 4 December 2017).

Lasisi. A., 'Experts Hail Nigerian Movie Industry at Cannes', *Punch*, 17 May 2018, https://punchng.com/experts-hail-nigerian-movie-industry-at-cannes/, (Accessed 6 June 2018).

Leadership, 'Dangote Group: Epitome of Good Corporate Governance', *Leadership Newspaper*, 12 June 2018, https://leadership.ng/2018/06/12/dangote-group-epitome-of-good-corporate-governance, (Accessed 17 July 2018).

Lewis, B. and Ross, A., 'Congo's 2017 Copper Up 7 CT Cobalt by 15 PCT', *Reuters*, 7 February 2018, https://www.reuters.com/article/africa-mining-congo-production/congos-2017-copper-output-up-7-pct-cobalt-by-15-pct-industry-idUSL8N1PX1EN, (Accessed 16 May 2018).

Lombard, L., *SAA Cargo Loses Top Spot as African Carrier to Ethiopian Airlines, Traveller24*, 29 April 2016, https://www.traveller24.com/News/Flights/saa-cargo-loses-top-spot-as-african-cargo-carrier-to-ethiopian-airlines-20160429, (Accessed 5 December 2017).

Longman, J., 'World Cup '98: France's Day of Soccer Glory Arrives; Upset of Brazil in World Cup', *The New York Times,* 13 July 1998, https://www.nytimes.com/1998/07/13/sports/world-cup-98-france-s-day-of-soccer-glory-arrives-upset-of-brazil-in-world-cup.html, (Accessed 25 November 2017).

Maasho, A. and Nako, M., 'Chad Signs Deal with Ethiopian Airlines to Launch Carrier', *Reuters,* 31 August 2018, https://www.standardmedia.co.ke/business/article/2001294487/chad-signs-deal-with-ethiopian-airlines-to-launch-carrier, (Accessed 11 September 2018).

Mangat, R., 'Behind the Scenes of 'Rafiki' at Cannes', *The East African,* 26 May 2018, http://www.theeastafrican.co.ke/magazine/Behind-the-scenes-of-Rafiki-at-Cannes/434746-4580450-y0ahon/index.html, (Accessed 11 September 2018).

Margolis, J., 'The Redeemed Church of God Preaches the Gospel in US', *BBC,* 12 February 2014, http://www.bbc.com/news/magazine-25988151, (Accessed 20 January 2018).

Mbodiam, B. R., 'Cameroon: Nexttel Exceeds 4 Million Subscribers in 3 years', *Business in Cameroon*, 18 November 2017, https://www.businessincameroon.com/telecom/1811-7570-cameroon-nexttel-exceeds-4-million-subscribers-in-3-years, (Accessed 10 May 2018).

Miserez, M., 'Collombey Refinery Closure – Dramatic Twist Means Tamoil Buyback May Be Possible', *SwissInfo*, 3 July 2015, http://www.swissinfo.ch/eng/business/collombey-refinery-closure_dramatic-twist-means-tamoil-buyback-may-be-possible/41529676, (Accessed 2 December 2017).

Muga, E., 'John Stephen Akhwari: Tanzania's Olympic Legend Who is Ignored at Home but Respected Globally', *All Africa*, 29 July 2012, https://allafrica.com/stories/201207290041.html, (Accessed 20 December 2017).

Mugisha, I.R. and Githaiga H., 'African Leaders Sign Largest Trade Treaty', *The East African,* 21 March 2018, http://www.theeastafrican.co.ke/business/African-leaders-sign-largest-trade-treaty-since-WTO/2560-4351410-7o1ix7/index.html, (Accessed 7 July 2018).

Mulupi, D., 'Keeping it in the Family: Manu Chandaria on the Value of Family Ties in Business', *How We Made It in Africa*, 15 October 2013, https://www.howwemadeitinafrica.com/keeping-it-in-the-family-manu-chandaria-on-the-value-of-family-ties-in-business/, (Accessed 8 September 2018).

Mulupi, D., 'NSIA Takes Over CDH Insurance', *Business and Finance,* [website], 23 February 2010, https://www.modernghana.com/news/265106/nsia-takes-over-cdh-insurance.html, (Accessed 3 January 2018).

Mumbere, D., 'Digital in 2018: Africa's internet users increase by 20%', *African News,* 6 February 2018, http://www.

africanews.com/2018/02/06/digital-in-2018-africa-s-internet-users-increase-by-20-percent/, (Accessed 14 March 2018).

Musyoki, J., 'One-Stop Border Posts Have Strengthened Cross-Border Trade', *The East African,* 8 March 2018, http://www.theeastafrican.co.ke/oped/comment/One-stop-border-posts-strengthen-cross-border-trade/434750-4334054-1jkc7vz/index.html, (Accessed 10 June 2018).

Neirotti, L. D., 'Offside! Is Rwanda sponsorship of Arsenal a flashy own goal?', *The East African,* 22 June 2018, http://www.theeastafrican.co.ke/oped/comment/Rwanda-sponsorship-of-Arsenal-a-flashy-own-goal/434750-4620808-35dc8ez/index.html, (Accessed 18 August 2018).

Njanja, A., 'Africa Accounts for 29pcs of Kenya's International Arrivals', *Business Daily,* 11 June 2018, https://www.businessdailyafrica.com/corporate/marketplace/Africa-Kenya-international-arrivals/4003114-4604900-xopjx3/index.html, (Accessed 11 June 2018).

Nsehe, M., 'Kenya Multimillionaire Says He Plans to List Some Companies', 9 April 2014, *Forbes,* https://www.forbes.com/sites/mfonobongnsehe/2014/04/09/kenyan-multimillionaire-manu-chandaria-says-he-plans-to-list-some-companies/#60f530586705, (Accessed 6 September 2018).

Nsehe, M., 'Nigerian Internet Enterpreneur Takes Nollywood to the World', *Forbes,* 16 August 2011, https://www.forbes.com/sites/mfonobongnsehe/2011/08/16/nigerian-internet-tycoon-takes-nollywood-to-the-.world/3/#f4f2072595d0, (Accessed 19 March 2018).

Nwabughiogu, L., 'Economic Downturn in Nigeria Affecting

Most African Nation - Beninoise', *Vanguard Nigeria,* 2 August 2016, https://www.vanguardngr.com/2016/08/nigeria-convert-gas-export-buhari/, (Accessed 28 January 2017).

Obura, F., 'South Africa's Shoprite Finalises Entry into Kenya's Retail Market', *Standard Media,* 27 February 2018, https://www.standardmedia.co.ke/business/article/2001271369/africa-s-biggest-grocer-to-open-seven-branches-in-kenya, (Accessed 8 March 2018).

Ohaeri, R. and K. Oyero, 'President Gnassingbe, African Ministers, Experts Push Frontiers on SAATM,' *Aviation Business Journal,* 11 June 2018, https://aviationbusinessjournal.aero/2018/06/11/president-gnassingbe-african-ministers-experts-push-frontiers-on-saatm/, (Accessed 15 August 2018).

Okonji, E., 'Skye9 Set to Drive Entertainment Industry with Digital Content', *This Day,* 19 January 2017, https://www.thisdaylive.com/index.php/2017/01/19/skye9-set-to-drive-entertainment-industry-with-digital-content/, (Accessed 14 February 2018).

Okoth, E., 'Kenya, Uganda trade thrives on one-stop border post in Busia', *Business Daily,* 26 April 2017, https://www.businessdailyafrica.com/magazines/Kenya-Uganda-trade-thrives-one-stop-border/1248928-3904116-fw4c3pz/index.html, (Accessed 7 April 2018).

Olingo, A., 'African Airline Flies High with Cargo on the Back of a Strong Economy', *The East African,* 14 August 2017, http://www.theeastafrican.co.ke/business/African-airlines-fly-high-with-cargo/2560-4056830-o6jklqz/index.html, (Accessed 3 September 2018).

Olingo, A., 'Ethiopian Airlines Poised to Take Over Africa's Skies', *The East African*, 19 August 2018, http://www.theeastafrican.co.ke/business/Ethiopian-Airlines-poised-to-take-over-Africa-skies/2560-4719056-l2u114z/index.html, (Accessed 14 September 2018).

Olingo, A., 'Ethiopian Carrier Flies High, Doubling Profits', *The East African*, 6 September 2017, http://www.theeastafrican.co.ke/business/Ethiopian-airlines-doubles-profits-/2560-4085128-8qwtef/index.html, (Accessed 7 October 2018).

Olowolagba, F., 'Ahmadu Bello University as Number One University in Nigeria', *Daily Post*, 17 December 2017, http://dailypost.ng/2017/12/17/ahmadu-bello-university-ranked-no-1-university-nigeria-see-full-list/, (Accessed 30 September 2018).

Onwuaso, U., 'Multichoice Plans Talent Factory Initiative', 11 June 2018, http://nigeriacommunicationsweek.com.ng/multichoice-plans-talent-factory-initiative/, (Accessed 5 February 2018).

Onyemaechi, I., 'Nigerian Short Film, 'Coat of Harm', to Premiere at Cannes', *The Cable LifeStyle*, 31 May 2017, https://lifestyle.thecable.ng/coat-harm-cannes-film-festival/, (Accessed 30 September 2018).

Oyetimi, K., 'Tourists Besiege Dominican Republic as TB Joshua Holds 2-Day Crusade', *Nigerian Tribune*, 27 November 2017, https://www.tribuneonlineng.com/120652/, (Accessed 29 November 2018).

Palmer, E., 'How Belgian Footballers Speak to One Another BBC', *The Standard*, 5 July 2018, https://www.bbc.com/news/world-europe-44624066, (Accessed 1 August 2018).

Rasmeni, M., 'Multichoice Talent Factory for the Creative Industry Launched', *Namibia Economist,* 31 May 2018, https://economist.com.na/35592/extra/multichoice-talent-factory-for-the-creative-industry-launched/, (Accessed 31 May 2018).

Reuters, 'OiLibya Buys Shell's Ethiopia, Djibouti Operations', 15 July 2008, *Reuters,* https://www.reuters.com/article/ethiopia-libya-shell/oilibya-buys-shells-ethiopia-djibouti-operations-idUSL159192220080715, (Accessed 17 October 2018).

Rioba, B., 'MultiChoice Launches Talent Factory Academy Targeting Film, TV Creatives', 31 May 2018, http://www.kbc.co.ke/multichoice-launches-talent-factory-academy-targeting-film-tv-creatives/, (Accessed 19 September 2018).

Saada, H., 'Forum of African Creators: Institution of the 'Miriam Makeba Prize for Artistic Creativity', 15 September 2017, http://www.aps.dz/culture/62837-forum-des-createurs-africains-institutiondu-prix-miriam-makeba-de-la-creativite-artistique, (Accessed 12 April 2018).

Safricom, 'Tax Hike on Mobile Money Will Hurt Industry', *The Standard,* 18 June 2018, p. 28.

Said, N., '2018 World Cup: Meet France's World Cup Players with Deep African Roots', *Times Live,* 1 January 2018, https://www.timeslive.co.za/sport/soccer/2018-07-01-meet-frances-world-cup-players-with-deep-african-roots/, (Accessed 14 June 2018).

Sasse, A. and P. Carsten, 'Nigeria Recession Deals Blow to Smuggling Hub Benin', *Reuters,* 30 March 2017, https://www.reuters.com/article/us-nigeria-benin-smuggling/

nigeria-recession-deals-blow-to-smuggling-hub-benin-idUSKBN17125X, (Accessed 16 October 2018).

Sisay, A., 'Sell Ethiopian Airlines Minority Stake to African Governments, CEO Urges', *The East African,* 19 August 2018, http://www.theeastafrican.co.ke/business/Ethiopian-Airlines-poised-to-take-over-Africa-skies/2560-4719056-l2u114z/index.html, (Accessed 1 October 2018).

Sococzynski, V., 'Nollywood 2.0: How Tech Is Making Africa's Movie Industry a Glabal Leader', *Venture Burn,* 12 November 2012, http://ventureburn.com/2012/11/nollywood-2-0-how-tech-is-making-africas-movie-industry-a-global-leader/, (Accessed 17 November 2017).

Strydom, T.J., 'South Africa's Shoprite to Accelerate African Expansion', 18 August 2015, https://af.reuters.com/article/investingNews/idAFKCN0QN0KW20150818?sp=true, (Accessed 8 March 2018).

Trustfull, P., 'Baba Ahmadou Danpullo Africa's Discreet Business Magnate', 1 February 2017, *World Finance,* https://www.worldfinance.com/markets/baba-ahmadou-danpullo-africas-discreet-business-magnate, (Accessed 11 May 2018).

Uduak, 'Top 8 Nigerian American Music Collaborations You Should Know', *Africa Music Law,* 6 August 2015, https://www.africamusiclaw.com/top-8-nigerian-american-music-collaborations-you-should-know/, (Accessed 12 May 2017).

UNICEF, 'Statistics', 'At a Glance: Nigeria', 2013, https://www.unicef.org/infobycountry/nigeria_statistics.html.

UNTWO, '2017 International Tourism Results: The Highest

in Seven Years', 15 January 2018, http://media.unwto.org/press-release/2018-01-15/2017-international-tourism-results-highest-seven-years, (Accessed 5 July 2018).

Wade, B. D., 'Jean Kacou Diagou (NSIA): <<Le Groupe NSIA N'Est Pas à Vendre', 24 April 2015, http://reussirbusiness.com/actualites/jean-kacou-diagou-nsia-le-groupe-nsia-nest-pas-a-vendre/, (Accessed 13 July 2018).

Xiaohuo, C., 'A Lasting Memory: Tanzanian Runner', *China Daily*, 1 November 2008, http://www.chinadaily.com.cn/olympics/2008-01/11/content_6388098.htm, (Accessed 16 September 2018).

Zaney, G.D., 'Ghana's Independence From Her Colonial Masters – Can It Be Meaningless?' *Government of Ghana*, http://www.ghana.gov.gh/index.php/media-center/features/3499-ghana-s-independence-from-her-colonial-masters-can-it-be-meaningless, (Accessed 7 February 2018).

'Abderrahman Samba Runs Second-Fastest 400m Hurdles Ever', *BBC Sport*, 1 July 2018, https://www.bbc.com/sport/av/athletics/44670453. (Accessed 17 May 2018).

'Afriqiyah Airways Focuses on Rebuilding Libya's Connectivity; International Capacity up 74% in October', *Anna Aero*, 24 October 2013, https://www.anna.aero/2013/10/24/afriqiyah-airways-focuses-on-rebuilding-libyas-connectivity/, (Accessed 3 October 2018).

'An Innovative Bank: Banque Nationale pour le Commerce et l'Industrie (BNCI)', https://history.bnpparibas/document/an-innovative-bank-banque-nationale-pour-le-commerce-et-lindustrie-bnci/, (Accessed 1 February 2018).

'Global Perspectives - Who Are the Leading Players?', *World Trade Statistical Review,* 2018, https://www.wto.org/english/res_e/statis_e/wts2018_e/wts2018chapter05_e.pdf, (Accessed 15 October 2018).

'How My Ministry is Boosting Tourism in Africa', *Thisday Newspapers,* 19 January 2018, http://www.thisdaylive.com/index.php/2018/01/19/how-my-ministry-is-boosting tourism-in-africa, (Accessed 3 March 2018).

'More Countries Sign the African Free Trade Agreement', *The East African,* 3 July 2018, http//www.theeastafrican.co.ke/business/African-free-trade-area-agreement-signing, (Accessed 17 August 2018).

'Multichoice Announces a Major Pan-African Initiative for Film and Television Industry', 30 May 2018, https://www.lusakatimes.com/2018/05/30/multichoice-announces-a-major-pan-african-initiative-for-film-television-industry/, (Accessed 4 July 2018).

'Prophet T.B. Joshua Visits Tanzania', *Tanzania Today,* http://www.tanzaniatoday.co.tz/news/prophet-tb-joshua-visits-tanzania, (Accessed 14 February 2018).

'RCCG to Build 3-km Long Auditorium', *Vanguard,* 10 August 2013, https://www.vanguardngr.com/2013/08/rccg-to-build-3-km-long-auditorium/, (Accessed 21 August 2017).

'Reports Link Ethiopian and DHL in Joint Venture', *Air Cargo News,* 9 July 2018, https://www.aircargonews.net/news/single-view/news/reports-link-ethiopian-and-dhl-in-joint-venture.html, (Accessed 14 May 2018).

'Running Low: The Story of Kenya's Blood Bank', *Daily Nation,* 12 June 2018, https://www.nation.co.ke/health/The-story-of-Kenyas-blood-bank/3476990-4606982-kxlg19/index.html, (Accessed 12 July 2018).

'South Africa: Cameroonian Snaps Up King's Court Bargain', 7 May 2010, http://www.postnewsline.com/2010/05/south-africa-cameroonian-snaps-up-kings-court-bargain.html, (Accessed 6 September 2017).

'South African Telcos Say Keen on "Attractive", Ethiopian Market', *Business Daily,* 8 June 2018, https://www.pressreader.com/kenya/business-daily-kenya/20180608/281861529199693, (Accessed 9 June 2018).

'Standard Trust Bank is Now UBA', *Ghana Web,* 23 January 2007, https://www.ghanaweb.com/GhanaHomePage/business/Standard-Trust-Bank-is-now-UBA-117754, (Accessed 25 December 2017).

'Tanzania Billionaires Buy Equity Bank Stake', *Business Daily,* 8 June 2018, p. 9.

'Tony Elumelu Foundation Selects 1000 Entrepreneurs For 2018', Programme, 22 March 2018, http://www.tonyelumelufoundation.org/news/tony-elumelu-foundation-selects-entrepreneurs-for-2018-programme/, (Accessed 3 April 2018).

'TradeMark East Africa Hands Over Busia, Uganda One Stop Border Post Facility. Operations Start', 9 June 2016, https://www.trademarkea.com/onestopborderposts/news_article/trademark-east-africa-hands-over-busia-uganda-one-stop-border-post-facility-operations-start/, (Accessed 4 March 2017).

'Viettel Cameroon to Operate under Nexttel Brand', 12 August 2014, *TeleGeography,* https://www.telegeography.com/products/commsupdate/articles/2014/08/12/viettel-cameroon-to-operate-under-nexttel-brand/, (Accessed 7 December 2017).

'We Have Produced More Local Content Than We Have Ever Done', *The Guardian Nigeria,* 10 August 2017, p. 43.

'Winners Chapel Has Six Million Members Spread Across 147 Countries - Oyedepo', 27 December 2014, *Vanguard,* https://www.vanguardngr.com/2014/12/winners-chapel-has-six-million-members-spread-across-147-countries-oyedepo/, (Accessed 5 January 2018).

INDEX

SECURE THE BASE

COMMENTARY BY NGŨGĨ WA THIONG'O

In *.Mind .Money. Matter: Pan- African Integration in the 21st Century,* Emeke E. Iweriebor .... looks at the strides already made towards ...a continent-wide integration. He addresses matters of trade, mobility between the countries and regions, banking and finance, industrialization and cultural industries. His inclusion of language and culture is important. Language is the primary storage of knowledge of a person's interaction with their environment. This generates culture which embodies values evolving from that interaction. These values form an individual and collective sense of self.

Drawing from his own banking experience, Iweriebor offers a practical way into our pan-African future. His is a practical vision. Pan-African integration is both the goal and the means of the continent becoming a secure base for all Africans. Enhancing the steps already taken towards this goal, and those further suggested in this book, are moves in the right direction.

Ngũgĩ Wa Thiong'o

This is a short but remarkable text by the most unusual of bankers – one who is not obsessed with short-term return in financial services but who understands the magic of value creation in the real economy, and the imperative of transformation through industrialisation and manufacturing. Emeke E. Iweriebor does not need lengthy chapters to make powerful points, share great knowledge, and distill wisdom. Like some grand music composers, he uses many variations on the single aria of integration to discuss the subtle ethics and the economics of togetherness. After exploring the main theme from various angles with different textures and harmonies, he brings back the original aria and gives it a unique feel from the first reading. The book is a well-informed report card, a travel diary, a seductive kaleidoscope, and a thoughtful meditation which will be of interest to a very large audience.

Célestin Monga
Visiting Professor of Public Policy
Harvard Kennedy School

POSTSCRIPT

As this edition of the book went to print, the state of affairs of public health globally, unraveled and a new world order emerged. In December 2019, a novel coronavirus disease 2019, globally known as COVID- 19 surreptitiously crept into the world. Discovered in Wuhan, in Hubei Province, in China, the pandemic raced and raged across the world, leaving devastation in its wake. The virus had varied symptoms, including flu, fever, sore throat, exhaustion, dry cough, pain, pneumonia, diarrhea, lack of smell, lack of taste, etc. The virus affected virtually all the regions, countries, and territories of the world.

For the first time in living memory, since the Spanish flu of 1918, nearly the entire world was shuttered with continents, countries, cities and communities, at varying times, and in varying degrees of lockdown and movement restrictions. Very sadly, as at July 2020, COVID - 19 had infected over 17.5 million people and killed over 675,000 people. It was a bad wave. With voluntary and mandatory usage of face coverings, social distancing, frequent washing of hands, other hygiene measures, effective vaccines and therapeutics, the management and treatment of COVID-19 will, expectedly, be mitigated

The pandemic immediately created or surfaced a lexicon of coronavirus, and reinforced interest in personal hygiene, epidemiology, and public health. Terms like testing, masks, gloves, physical distancing, social distancing, contact tracing, isolation, quarantine, climbing the curve, flattening the curve, anti-body test, in-person, asymptomatic, pre-symptomatic, symptomatic, essential workers, first responders, herd immunity, containment, and others became words and phrases of frequent use and widespread familiarity.

IMPACT

The spread, disruption, destruction and death occasioned by the pandemic has had a deep and negative impact on public health, national economies, international trade, in-country and international travels, the global financial system, and many more. Economies unraveled; companies collapsed; and, millions of employees lost their jobs. It also accelerated the digitalization of various aspects of life, as technology facilitated more activities without in-person presence. Virtual meetings, video and audio conferencing, webinars, etc became the norm, and the businesses of the providers of these services blossomed. In the US, for example, the state of New York, even legalized virtual weddings.

On the flip side, COVID-19 revealed again that diseases, outbreaks, epidemics, and pandemics, more often than not, have differential impacts on individuals, groups and communities. Diseases are not equal opportunity attackers, but re-inforce the symbiotic relationship between economic and social inequalities, public health, survival and living.

WAY FORWARD

In 2020, the world witnessed rapid and unprecedented change. Individuals, corporates, governments, communities, countries, not-for-profit and international multilateral organizations, etc, must take concerted measures to protect citizens from the overwhelming scourge and devastating effects, of an epidemic, or a pandemic, in future.

ACKNOWLEDGEMENTS

Writing this book has challenged and inspired me.

Grinding out the time, especially at odd hours to construct words, lines and pages was arduous, but fulfilling. Many times, I stopped writing for days, weeks and months and asked myself, *why am I doing all this?* Nonetheless, I persisted. I was determined to finish the book as I felt strongly that the expressed ideas, thoughts and views are potent and living. They deserve to be read and heard.

I am profoundly grateful to my family for the kindness and constant support. Charles, Obuse-Oje, Gayla, Ehiedu, Pearl, Bridget, Martins, Hadiza, Owanta, Adi, Betty, Nduka and James as well as Iyare II, Ebere, Ehika, Nwanua, Nneka, Fanon, Philip, Victoria, Abu, Gabrielle, Damilola, Victory, Segun, Bamaiyi and Prince. My family nurtured my early interest in, and commitment to, pan-African affairs, education and scholarship. Professor Ehiedu E. G. Iweriebor firmly insisted that this was a distinct story that had to be told. I remain grateful for his rich vein of ideas on the evolution and development of societies. He read the work, guided me and walked me through his well- trodden path.

To my wife Eleojo Erere, I remain deeply appreciative of the ready support and sacrifice. She encouraged and prodded me to *finish this book.* My children, Elurinmakiwehe Ehieroke, Elumedon Titi and

Iyare III Elurinhunkahunriazun were of great help. Their time and forbearance were invaluable. Without them all, the book would not have been completed.

In all, I thank God for making this possible.

Lightning Source UK Ltd.
Milton Keynes UK
UKHW010631011020
370850UK00001B/48